"The divorce. There is a complication."

"What complication?" she asked, suspicious, though her traitorous body did not seem to care. It throbbed for him, hot and needy.

"I am afraid that it cannot be done remotely." He shrugged in that supremely Italian way, as if to say that the vagaries of such things were beyond anyone's control, even his.

"You cannot mean…" she began. His gaze found hers then, so very dark and commanding, and she felt goose bumps rise along her arms, her neck. As if someone walked across her grave, she thought distantly.

"There is no getting around it," he said, but his voice was not apologetic. His gaze was direct. And Bethany went completely cold. "I am afraid that you must return to Italy."

All about the author...
Caitlin Crews

CAITLIN CREWS discovered her first romance novel at the age of twelve. It involved swashbuckling pirates, grand adventures, a heroine with rustling skirts and a mind of her own, and a seriously mouthwatering and masterful hero. The book (the title of which remains lost in the mists of time) made a serious impression. Caitlin was immediately smitten with romances and romance heroes, to the detriment of her middle-school social life. And so began her lifelong love affair with romance novels, many of which she insists on keeping near her at all times.

Caitlin has made her home in places as far-flung as York, England, and Atlanta, Georgia. She was raised near New York City, and fell in love with London on her first visit when she was a teenager. She has backpacked in Zimbabwe, been on safari in Botswana and visited tiny villages in Namibia. She has, while visiting the place in question, declared her intention to live in Prague, Dublin, Paris, Athens, Nice, the Greek Islands, Rome, Venice and/or any of the Hawaiian islands. Writing about exotic places seems like the next best thing to moving there.

She currently lives in California, with her animator/comic-book artist husband and their menagerie of ridiculous animals.

Other titles by Caitlin Crews available in ebook:

Harlequin Presents®

Caitlin Crews
PRINCESS FROM THE PAST

TORONTO NEW YORK LONDON
AMSTERDAM PARIS SYDNEY HAMBURG
STOCKHOLM ATHENS TOKYO MILAN MADRID
PRAGUE WARSAW BUDAPEST AUCKLAND

Recycling programs
for this product may
not exist in your area.

ISBN-13: 978-0-373-23814-9

PRINCESS FROM THE PAST

First North American Publication 2012

Copyright © 2011 by Caitlin Crews

www.Harlequin.com

Printed in U.S.A.

PRINCESS FROM THE PAST

CHAPTER ONE

BETHANY Vassal did not have to turn around. She knew exactly who had just entered the exclusive art-gallery in Toronto's glamorous Yorkville neighborhood. Even if she had not heard the increased buzz from the well-clad, cocktail-sipping crowd, or felt the sudden spike in energy roll through the long, bright space like an earthquake, she would have known. Her body knew and reacted immediately. The back of her neck prickled in warning. Her stomach tensed. Her muscles clenched tight in automatic response. She stopped pretending to gaze at the bold colors and twisted shapes of the painting before her and let her eyes drift closed to ward off the memories. And the pain—so much pain.

He was here. After all this time, after all her agonizing, planning and years of isolation, he was in the same room. She told herself she was ready.

She had to be.

Bethany turned slowly. She had deliberately situated herself in the furthest corner of the upscale gallery so she could see down the gleaming wood and white corridor to the door, so she could prepare herself when he arrived. But the truth, she was forced to admit to herself as she finally twisted all the way around to face the inevitable commotion near the great glass doors, was that there was really no way to prepare. Not for Prince Leopoldo Di Marco.

Her husband.

Soon to be ex-husband, she told herself fiercely. If she told herself the same thing long enough, it had to become true, didn't it? It had nearly killed her to leave him three years ago, but this was different. She was different.

She had been so broken when she'd met him—still reeling from the death of the bedridden father she'd cared for through his last years; still spinning wildly in the knowledge that suddenly, at twenty-three, she could have any life she wanted instead of being a sick man's care-giver. Except she hadn't known what to want. The only world she'd ever known had been so small. She had been grieving—and then there had been Leo, like a sudden bright sunrise after years of rain.

She'd believed he was perfect, the perfect prince out of a story book. And she'd believed that with him she was some kind of fairy-tale princess who could escape into the perfect dream come true. Bethany's mouth twisted. She'd certainly learned better, hadn't she? He'd smashed that belief into pieces by abandoning her in every way that mattered once they'd reached his home in Italy. By shutting her out, leaving her more alone than she had ever been before, overwhelmed and lonely half a world away from all she'd ever known.

And then he'd decided he wanted to bring a child into all of that despair. It had been impossible, the final straw. Bethany's hands clenched at her sides as if she could strike out at her memories. She forced herself to take a deep breath. Anger would not help her now—only focus. She had very specific goals tonight. She wanted her freedom, and she could not allow herself to get sidetracked by the past.

Then she looked up and saw him. The world seemed to contract and then expand around her. Time seemed to stop—or perhaps that was simply her ability to draw breath.

He strode through the gallery, flanked by two stone-faced members of his security detail. He was, as he had always been, a heartbreaking study of dark-haired, gleaming-eyed Italian male beauty. He wore, with nonchalant ease, an elegantly tailored dark suit that somehow made him seem even more ruggedly handsome than he naturally was. It clung to his broad shoulders and showcased his mouth-watering physique.

But Bethany could not allow herself to focus on his physicality; it was too dangerous. She had forgotten, somehow, that he was so…vivid. Her memory had made him smaller, duller. It had muted the sheer force of him, making her forget how commanding he was, how his uncompromising masculinity and irrefutable power seemed to radiate from him, making everyone in his vicinity both step back and stare.

It also made her profoundly sad. She swallowed and tried to shake the melancholy away. It could not possibly help her here.

His long, tall, exquisitely hewn body, was all rangy muscle and sensual male grace, moving through the crowd with a kind of liquid ease. His cheekbones were high and pronounced—noticeable from across a large room. He carried himself as if he were a king or a god. His mouth, even in its current flat, disapproving line, hinted at the shattering sensuality she knew far too well he could and would use as his most devastating weapon against her. His rich, thick, dark-brown hair was cut to suit perfectly the ruthless, focused magnate she knew him to be—whatever else he might be.

Everything he wore, even the way he held

himself, broadcasted his wealth, his power, and that dark, sexual magnetism that was uniquely his. It was as much a part of him as his olive skin, his corded muscles and his earthy, woodsy scent—which she must be remembering, she told herself, frowning, for she was certainly not close enough to him to smell his skin. Nor would she be ever again, she vowed.

For he was no fairy tale prince, as she had once so innocently imagined. Bethany had to bite back a hollow laugh. There were no swelling, happy songs, no happily-ever-afters—not with Leo Di Marco, *Principe di Felici*. Bethany had learned that the hardest, most painful way possible. His was an ancient and revered title, with ancient responsibilities and immutable duties, and Leo was its steward. First, foremost, always, he was the title.

She watched his dark eyes flick through the crowd with ruthless impatience. He looked annoyed. Already. She sucked in a shaky breath. Then, inevitably, he found her. She felt the kick of his gaze like a punch to her gut and had to breathe through the sudden light-headedness. She had wanted this, she reminded herself. She had to see this through now, finally, or she did not know what might become of her.

Bethany had to force herself to stand up straight, to simply wait there as he bore down on her. She crossed her arms, held on tight to her elbows and tried to look unmoved by his approach even as she quaked with that inevitable, unfair reaction to his presence that had always ruined her attempts to stand up to him before. Meanwhile memories she refused to delve into haunted her still, flickering across her mind too quickly, leaving the same old scars behind.

Leo dismissed his bodyguards with the barest flick of a finger, his dark gaze fused to hers, his long legs eating up the distance between them. He looked overpowering and overwhelming, as he always had, as he always would—as if he alone could block out the rest of the world. Worst of all, she knew he could. And would. And did.

Bethany's throat was too dry. She had the overwhelming urge to turn away, to run, but she knew he would only follow. More than that, it would defeat her purpose. She had chosen this particular meeting-place deliberately: a bright and crowded art-opening filled with the sort of people who would recognize a man of Leo's stature at a glance. Protection, she had thought, as much from Leo's inevitable fury as from her own ungovernable response to this man.

This would not be like the last time. He had

been so angry and she had foolishly thought that maybe they might work something out—if he'd actually spoken to her for once, instead of putting her off. Three years had passed since that night, and still, thinking of the things he had said and the way it had all exploded into that devastating, unwanted and uncontainable passion, that still shamed her to remember—

She shoved the memories aside and squared her shoulders.

Then he was right there in front of her, his gaze taut on hers. She could not breathe.

Leo.

Already, after mere seconds, that heady, potent masculinity that was his and his alone pulled her in, tugging at parts of her she'd thought long dead. Already she felt that terrible, familiar yearning swell within her, urging her to move closer, to bury herself in the heat of him, to lose herself in him as she nearly had before.

But she was different now. She'd had to be to survive him. She was no longer the naïve, weak little girl he had handled so carelessly throughout the eighteen harrowing months of their marriage. The girl with no boundaries and no ability to stand up for herself.

She would never be that girl again. She had worked too hard three years ago to leave her behind. To grow into the woman she should have been all along.

Leo merely stared at her, his dark, coffee-colored eyes narrowing slightly, as bitter and black as she remembered. He would have looked indolent, almost bored, were it not for the faintest hint of grim tension in his lean jaw and the sense of carefully leashed power that hummed just beneath his skin.

"Hello, Bethany," he said, his sardonic voice richer, deeper than she'd remembered.

Her name in his cruel mouth felt…intimate. It mocked her with the memories she refused to acknowledge, yet still seemed to affect her breathing, her skin, her heartbeat.

"What game are you playing tonight?" he asked softly, his eyes dark and unreadable, his voice controlled. "I am touched that you thought to include me after all this time."

She could not let him cow her; she could not let him shake her. Bethany knew it was now or never. She clenched her hands tighter around her elbows, digging her fingers deep into her own flesh.

"I want a divorce," she said, tilting back her head to look at him directly.

She had planned and practiced those words for so long in her mirror, in her head, in every spare moment, that she knew she sounded just as she wished to sound: calm, cool, resolute. There was no hint at all of the turmoil that rolled inside of her.

The words seemed to hang there in the space between their bodies. Bethany kept her gaze trained on Leo's, ignoring the hectic color she could feel scratching at her neck and pretending she was not at all affected by the way he seemed to go very still as he looked at her with narrowed eyes. As if he was gathering himself to pounce. Bethany's heart pounded as if she'd screamed that single sentence loud enough to shatter glass, shred clothing and perhaps even rebound off the top of the iconic CN Tower to deafen the entire city.

It was the man standing much too close to her. Leo was next to her, so close she could nearly feel the waves of heat and arrogance emanate from him. Leo, watching her with those intense, unreadable eyes. It made something deep inside of her flex and coil. Leo was the husband she had once loved so destructively, so desperately, when she did not know enough to love herself. It made her want to weep as that same old sadness washed through her, reminding her of all the ways they had failed each other. But no more. No more.

Her stomach was a tense, clenched ball. Her palms were damp. She had to fight to keep her vision clear, her eyes bland. She had to order herself repeatedly not to heed her body's urgent demand that she wrench her gaze away and flee.

Indifference, she reminded herself. She must show him nothing but indifference, however feigned it might be. Anything but that, and all would be lost. She would be lost.

"It is a great pleasure to see you too," Leo said finally with an unmistakable edge in his voice. His English had a distinctly British intonation that spoke of his years of education, with the sensual caress of his native Italian beneath. His dark eyes gleamed with cold censure as they flicked over her, taking in the careful chignon that tamed her dark-brown curls, her minimal cosmetics, the severe black suit. She had worn it to convince them both that this was nothing more than a bit of unpleasant business—and because it helped conceal her figure from his appraisal. She was a far cry from the girl he had once memorably brought to climax with no more than his hot, demanding gaze, and still he made her want to squirm. Still, she felt brushfires blaze to life in every place his dark gaze touched her.

She hated what he could do to her even now, after everything. As if three years later her body still had not received the message that they were finished.

Leo continued, his voice dangerously even, his gaze like steel. "I do not know why it should surprise me in the least that a woman who would behave as you have done should greet your husband in such a fashion."

She could not let him see that he rattled her still, when she had thought—prayed—that she'd put all that behind her. But she told herself she could worry about what that might mean later, at her leisure, when she had the years ahead of her to process all the things she felt about this man. When she was free of him.

And she had to be free of him. It was finally time to live her own life on her own terms. It was time to give up that doomed, pathetic hope she was embarrassed to admit she harbored that he would keep his angry promise to come after her and drag her back home if she dared leave him. He had come that one terrible night and then left again, telling her in no uncertain terms of her importance to him. It was three years past time to accord him the same courtesy.

"You will forgive me if I did not think the social niceties had any place here," she said instead as calmly as she could, as if she could not feel that sharp gaze of his leaving marks on her skin. "Given our circumstances."

Bethany had to move then, or explode. She walked toward the next bright, jumbled canvas on the stark-white wall and sensed instead of saw Leo keep pace with her. When she stopped moving, he was beside her once again, close enough that she could almost feel his heat, the corded strength in his arm. Close enough that she was tempted to lean into him.

At least now she could control her destructive impulses, she thought bitterly, even if she could not quite rid herself of those urges as she'd like.

"Our 'circumstances,'" he echoed after a tense, simmering moment, his voice dark and sinful, at odds with the razor's edge beneath. "Is that what you call it? Is that how you rationalize your actions?" A quick sideways glance confirmed that one dark brow was raised, mocking and cruel, matching his tone perfectly. Bethany knew that expression all too well. A chill moved through her.

She was aware of her own pulse drumming wildly in her veins and had to stop herself from fidgeting with the force of will that, three years ago, she had not known she possessed. But it had been forged day by day in the bright fire of his cold indifference. At least she knew it existed now, and that she could use it.

"It does not matter what you wish to call it," she said, fighting to remain cool. She turned toward him and wished at once that she had not. He was too big, too male, too much. "It is obviously time that both of us moved on."

She did not care for the way that Leo watched her then, his eyes hooded, predatory. They reminded her exactly how dangerous this man was and exactly why she had left him in the first place.

"This is why you deigned to contact me tonight?" he asked in a deceptively soft voice that sent a chill spiraling down her spine. "To discuss a divorce?"

"Why else would I contact you?" she asked, wanting her voice to sound careless, light, but hearing all too well that it was tight with anxiety.

"I can think of no other reason, of course," he said, his eyes fixed on her in a way that made her deeply uncomfortable down into her very bones. She set her jaw and refused to look away. "Certainly I knew better than to imagine that you might finally be ready to resume your duties or keep your promises. And yet here I am."

She did not know how long she could keep this up. He was too overwhelming, too impossible. She had been unable to handle him when he had been as lost in the volcanic passion between them as she was. But his anger, his lacerating coldness, was much, much worse. She was not certain she was equal to it. She was not at all sure she could pretend not to be wounded by it.

"I do not want anything from you except this divorce," Bethany forced herself to say.

Her body was staging a civil war. One part wanted to run for the door and disappear into the chilly fall evening. What was truly distressing and shocking was that part of her did not. Part of her instead ached for his hands that she knew could wield such dark sorcery against her flesh. She did not want to think about that. To remember. Touching Leo Di Marco was like leaping head-first into the sun. She would not survive it a second time. She would feel too much, he would feel too little and she would be the one to pay the price. She knew it as well as she knew her own name.

She straightened her shoulders, and made herself look at him directly, as if she were truly brave instead of desperate. Did it really matter which? "I want to be done with this farce, Leo."

"And to what farce, exactly, do you refer?" he asked silkily, thrusting his hands into the pockets of his trousers, his gaze fixed on her face in a way that made her want to fidget. It made her feel scorched from the inside out. "When you ran away from me, from our marriage and our home, and relocated halfway across the globe?"

"That was not a farce," she dared to say. There was no longer anything to lose, and she could not give in to her own desolation. "It was a fact."

"It is a disgrace," he said, his voice deceptively quiet, though she did not mistake the cold ferocity and hard lash of it. "But why speak of such things? You prove with your every breath that you have no interest at all in the shame you bring upon my family, my name."

"Which is why we must divorce," Bethany said, fighting to keep the edge from her voice and failing. "Problem solved."

"Tell me something," he said. With a peremptory jerk of his chin, he dismissed a hovering gallery-worker bearing a tray of champagne flutes then returned his gaze to Bethany's. "Why this particular step? And why now? It has been three years since you abandoned me."

"Since I escaped, you mean," she retorted without thinking, and knew as soon as the words had passed her lips that she had made a grave error.

His dark eyes flared with heat and she felt an answering fire rage through her. It was as potent as the sense of being nothing more to him than prey, but she could not allow herself to look away.

She could not allow him to railroad her into another bargain with the devil made out of desperation and, cruelest of all, that tiny flicker of hope that nothing had ever managed to stamp out—not even his disinterest. She had to be out from under his thumb.

For good.

Prince Leo Di Marco told himself he was coldly, deeply furious. But it was no more than anger, no more than righteous indignation, he assured himself; it went no deeper than that. This woman's uncanny ability to sneak around his lifelong armor and wound him was a thing of the past. It had to be.

He had spent the whole of his day in meetings on Bay Street, Toronto's financial center. There was not a banker or businessman there who dared challenge the ancient Di Marco name—much less the near-limitless funds that went with it. Bethany was the only woman who had ever defied him, who had ever hurt him. The only person that he could remember doing so.

Three years on and she was doing it still. He had to fight himself to maintain his controlled exterior. He could feel the anger that only she inspired in him opening up that great, black cavern within him that he had long preferred to ignore. He knew exactly why she had demanded they meet in a public place—as if he was some kind of wild animal. As if he needed to be contained. Handled. He was not certain why this insult, atop all the others, should bite at him so deeply.

It infuriated him that he was not immune to her fresh-faced beauty that had so captivated and deceived him in the first place. She was still far too much of a temptation. Her angelic blue eyes were such an intriguing contrast to her dark-brown curls, all of it tempered with the faintest spray of freckles across her pert nose. He did not allow himself to concentrate on the delicate fullness of her mouth. It did not seem to matter that he knew her appearance of wide-eyed innocence was nothing more than an act.

It never seemed to matter.

He wanted his hands on her skin, his mouth on her breast. Those tight, ripe nipples against his tongue. He told himself it was all he wanted, all he chose to allow himself to want.

"Escaped?" he queried, icily. "The last I checked, you were living quite comfortably. In a house I own."

"Because you demanded it!" she hissed,

that fascinating splash of color rising from her graceful neck toward her soft cheeks. He knew other ways to raise that color upon her delicate skin and very nearly smiled, remembering. She darted a glance around at the crowd which surrounded them, as if for strength, then faced him again. "I wanted nothing to do with that house."

He was a man who commanded empires. He had done so since his father's death when he was only twenty-eight, maintaining his family's ancient wealth while expanding it into the new era. How could this one woman continue to defy him? How was it possible? What weakness in him kept him from simply crushing her beneath his foot?

But he already knew the weakness intimately. It had already ruined him. He felt it in the heaviness in his groin, the edgy need that spiraled through him and demanded he get his hands beneath the heavy black suit he knew she was wearing to hide from him. Because she could never deny what she felt when he touched her, that he knew full well. Whatever else she chose to deny, or he preferred to ignore.

"I am fascinated by your uncharacteristic acquiescence," he said through his teeth, furious with himself and with their entire tangled history, her trail of broken promises. "I recall making any number of demands that you chose to ignore: that you remained in Italy, as tradition required. That you refrained from casting shame on my family's name with your behavior. That you honored your vows."

"I will not fight with you," she told him, her blue eyes flashing and her chin rising. She made a dismissive gesture with one hand, the one that should have worn his ring yet was offensively bare. He clamped down on the surge of temper. "You can choose to revise history however you like, but I am finished arguing about it."

"Then we are in perfect agreement," he bit out, keeping his voice low and for her ears alone despite the fierce kick of his temper—and that hollow place beneath it that he refused to acknowledge. "I have not gained an appreciation for public scenes since we last met, Bethany. If it is your plan to embarrass me further tonight, I suggest you rethink it. I do not think this will end the way you wish it to end."

"There is no need for a scene," she said at once. "Public or otherwise." She shrugged, drawing attention to her delicate neck, and reminding him of the kisses he'd once pressed there and the sweet, addictive taste of her skin. But it was as if that was from another life. "I only want to be divorced from you. Finally."

"Because it has been such a hardship for you

to stay married to me?" he asked, his voice cutting and sarcastic. "How you must struggle."

He was not a man who believed in impassioned displays—particularly in public, where he was forever being held up against the example of his family's long legacy—but this woman had always provoked him like no other. Tonight her eyes were too blue, her mouth set in too firm a line. It clawed at him.

"I understand how it must cut at you," he continued coldly. "To live in such unearned luxury. To have all the benefits of my name and protection with none of the attendant responsibilities."

"You will be pleased to learn that I no longer want them, then," she said. She raised her brows at him in direct challenge, but he was caught by the flash of vulnerability he saw move across her face. Bethany—vulnerable? That was not a word he'd ever use to describe her. Wild. Uncontrollable. Rebellious. But never defenseless, wounded. Never.

Impatiently, Leo shoved the odd turn of thought aside. The last thing in the world he needed now was to become intrigued anew by his wife. He had yet to recover from the initial disaster that had been his first, ruinous fascination with this woman. Look where it had led them both.

"Do you not?" he asked, his voice harsh, directed as much at his errant thoughts as at her. "How can you be certain when you have treated both with such disrespect?"

"I want a divorce," she said again with a quiet strength. "This is the end, Leo. I'm moving on with my life."

"Are you?" he asked, his tone dangerous. She either did not hear it or did not care. "How so?"

"I am moving out of that house," she said at once, a wild fire he could not entirely comprehend raging in her sky-blue eyes. "I hate it. I never wanted to live there in the first place."

"You are my wife." His voice cracked like a whip, though he knew the words had long held no meaning for her, no matter that they still moved through him like blood, like need. "Whether you choose to acknowledge it or not. Just because you have turned your back on the vows you made, does not mean that I have. I told you I would protect you and I meant it, even if it is from your own folly and stubborn recklessness."

"I'm sure you think that makes you some kind of hero," she threw at him in a falsely polite tone that he knew was for the benefit of the crowd around them. Yet he could see the real Bethany burn bright in her eyes and the flush on her neck. "But I never thought anyone was likely to kidnap me in the first place." She let out a short, hollow laugh. "Believe me, I do not advertise our connection."

"And yet it exists." His voice brooked no argument; it could have melted steel. "And because of it, you are a target."

"I won't be for much longer," she said, her foolhardy determination showing in that stubborn set to her jaw and the fire in her eyes. He almost admired it. Almost. "And you'll find that I've never touched any of the money in that account of yours, either. I'm going to walk out of this marriage exactly as I walked into it."

"And where do you intend to go?" he asked quietly, softly, not daring himself to move closer. He knew, somehow, that putting his hands on her would ruin them both and expose too much.

"Not that it's any of your business," she said, her gaze direct and challenging, searing into him. "But I've met someone else."

CHAPTER TWO

THE room seemed to drop away. All Bethany could see was the arrested look in his eyes that narrowed as he gazed at her. He did not move, yet she felt clenched in a kind of tight fist that held only the two of them, and that simmering tension that sparked and surged between them.

Had she really said that? Had she truly dared to say something like that to this man? To her husband?

How much worse would it be, she wondered in a panic, if it was actually true? She found she was holding her breath.

For a long, impossible moment Leo only stared at her, but she could feel the beat of his fury—and her own heart—like a wild drum. He looked almost murderous for a moment—or perhaps she was succumbing to hysteria. Then he shifted, and Bethany could breathe again.

"And who is the lucky man?" Leo asked in a lethally soft voice. When she only stared at him, afraid that her slightest movement might act as a red flag before a bull, his head tilted slightly to the left, though he did not lift his dark eyes from hers. "Your lover?"

Bethany somehow kept herself from shivering. It was the way he'd said that word. It seemed to skate over her skin, dangerous and deadly. She already regretted the lie. She knew she had only said it to hit at him, to hurt him in some small way—to get inside that iron control of his and make him as uncertain and unsettled as she always felt in his presence. To show him that she was deadly serious about divorcing him. Why had she sunk to his level?

But then she remembered who she was dealing with. Leo would say anything—do anything—to get what he wanted. She must be as ruthless as he was; if he had taught her nothing else, he had taught her that.

"We met at university while I finished my degree," she said carefully, searching his hard features for some sign of what might happen next, or some hint of the anger she suspected lurked just out of sight beneath those cold eyes.

She reminded herself that the point was to end this tragedy of a marriage once and for all. Why should she feel as if she should go easy, as if she should protect Leo in some way? When had he ever protected her—from anything?

"He is everything I want in a man," she said boldly. Surely some day she would meet someone who fit that bill? Surely she deserved that much? "He is considerate. Communicative. As interested in my life as in his own."

Unlike Leo, who had abandoned his young wife entirely the moment they'd reached Italy, claiming his business concerns were far more pressing. Unlike Leo, who had closed himself off completely and had been coldly dismissive, when Bethany had not been able to understand why the man who had once adored her in every possible way had disappeared. Unlike Leo, who had thrown around words like 'responsibility' and 'duty' but had only meant that Bethany should follow his orders without question.

Unlike Leo, who had used the powerful sexual chemistry between them like a weapon, keeping her addicted, desperate and yet so very lonely for far longer than she should have been.

Something flared in the depths of his dark gaze then, something that shimmered through her, arrowing straight to her core, coiling tight and hot inside of her. It was as if he knew exactly what she was remembering and was remembering it too. Their bodies twined together, their skin slick and warm, their mouths fused—and Leo thrusting deep inside her again and again.

She took a ragged breath, jerked her gaze away from his and tried to calm her thudding heart. Those memories had no place here, now. There was no point to them. Leo had not destroyed her, as he'd seemed so bent on doing. She had survived. She had left him, and all that remained was this small legal matter. She would have spoken only to his staff about it and avoided this meeting, had they not insisted that the principe would wish to deal with this, with her, personally.

"He sounds like quite the paragon," Leo replied after a long moment, much too calmly. He raised his dark brows slightly when she frowned at him.

"He is," Bethany said firmly, wondering why she felt so unbalanced, as if she was being childish somehow—instead of using the only weapon she could think of that might actually do more than bounce off of him. Perhaps it was simply that being near Leo now made her feel as she had felt when she'd been with him: so very young and silly. Naïve and foolish.

"Far be it from me to stand in the way of such a perfect union," Leo murmured, running his hand along the front of his exquisite suit jacket as if it required smoothing. As if anything he wore would dare defy him and wrinkle!

Bethany's frown deepened. That was too blatant, surely? "There is no need for sarcasm."

"I must contact my attorneys," Leo said, his dark eyes hard on hers. Bethany felt slightly dizzy as that familiar old fire licked through her, making her legs tremble beneath her and her breath tangle in her throat.

How unfair that he could still affect her so after everything that had happened! Yet there was a part of her that knew that it was safer to acknowledge the attraction than the grief that lurked beneath it.

"Your attorneys?" she echoed, knowing she had to say something. She knew she could not simply stare at him with that impossible yearning welling up within her for the man he could never be, the man he was not.

She wished suddenly that she had more experience. That she had not been so sheltered and out of her depth when she'd met Leo. As if she'd spent her youth hermetically sealed away, which of course, in many ways, she had. But how could she have done anything else? There had been no one but Bethany to nurse her father through his long, extended illness; no one but Bethany to administer what care she could until his eventual death.

But she had had to drop out of her second year of university to do it when she was barely nineteen. She had been twenty-three when she'd met Leo on that fateful trip to her father's favorite place in the world, Hawaii. She had dutifully traveled with the small inheritance he'd left behind to spread his ashes in the sea, as he'd wished. How could she have been prepared for an honest-to-goodness prince?

She had hardly imagined such creatures existed outside of fiction. She had been utterly off-balance from the moment he'd looked at her with those deep, dark eyes that had seemed to brand her from the inside out. Maybe if she'd been more like other girls her age, if she'd been more mature, if she'd ventured out from the tiny little world her father's needs had dictated she make her own...

But there was no use trying to change the past—and, anyway, Bethany could not begrudge the years she'd spent caring for her father. She could only move forward now, armed with the strength she had not possessed at twenty-three. She had been artless and unformed then, and Leo had flattened her. That would never happen again.

"Yes," he said now, his gaze moving over her face as if he could see the very things she so desperately wished to keep hidden: her lies. Her bravado. That deep despair at what they'd made of their marriage. That tiny spark of hope she would give anything to extinguish, once and for all. "My attorneys must handle any divorce proceedings, of course. They will let me know what is involved in such a matter." His smile was thin, yet still polite. Barely. "I have no experience with such things."

Bethany was confused and wary. Was this really happening? Was he simply caving? Agreeing? She had not imagined such a thing could be possible. She had imagined he would fight, and fight dirty. Not because he wanted her, of course, but because he was not a man who had ever been left, and his pride would demand he fight. She was not certain what the hollow feeling that washed through her meant.

"Is this a trick?" she asked after a moment.

Leo's brows lifted with pure, male arrogance. He looked every inch the scion of a noble bloodline that he was.

"A trick?" he repeated, as if he was unfamiliar with the term yet found it vaguely distasteful.

"You were opposed to my leaving you in the first place," she pointed out stiffly. That was a vast understatement. "And you did not seem any more resigned to the idea of it tonight. How can I trust that you will really do this?"

He did not speak for a long moment, yet that simmering awareness between them seemed to reach boiling point. Once again, Bethany felt heat and a deep, encompassing panic wash over her. She thought he almost smiled then.

Instead, he reached over and took her hand in his impossibly warm, hard grasp.

Flames raced up her arm, and she felt her whole body tighten in reaction. She felt the ache of it, both physical and, worse, emotional. She wanted to yank her hand from his more than she wanted to draw her next breath, but she forced herself to stand still, to let him touch her, to pretend she was unmoved by the feel of his skin against hers.

Leo watched her for a moment then dropped his brooding gaze to her hand. His thumb moved back and forth over the backs of her fingers, sending sensation streaking through her. She felt herself melt for him, as she always had at even his slightest touch. She ached—and she hated him for it.

"What are you doing?" she managed to say through lips that hardly moved. How could she still be so helpless? How could he have this power over her?

"You seem to have misplaced your wedding ring," he said quietly, still looking at her hand, the chill in his voice in direct contrast to the bright, hot flame of his touch.

"I did not misplace it," she gritted out. "I removed it a long time ago. Deliberately."

"Of course you did," he murmured, and then murmured something else in Italian that she was delighted not to understand.

"I thought about pawning it," she continued, knowing that would bring his gaze back to hers. She raised her brows. "But that would be petty."

"And you are many things, Bethany, are you not?" His mouth was so grim, his eyes a dark blaze. He let her hand go and she pulled it back too quickly, too obviously. His mouth twisted, mocking her. "But never petty."

Leo stared out the floor-to-ceiling window of the penthouse condominium that had been secured for his use. But he did not see the towers of Bay Street, nor the muted lights of downtown Toronto still glittering at his feet despite the late hour.

He could not sleep. He told himself it was because he hated the inevitable rain, the cold and the wet that swept in from Lake Ontario that chilled to the bone and yet passed for autumn in this remote, northern place. He told himself he needed nothing but another drink—perhaps that might ease the tension that still ravaged through him.

But he could not seem to get Bethany's bright

blue eyes, clear and challenging, out of his head. And then that flash of vulnerability, as if she'd hurt—and deeply.

She was like some kind of witch.

He had thought so when they had collided in the warm, silky surf off of Waikiki Beach. He had caught her in his arms to keep her from tumbling with the breakers toward the sand, and it had been those eyes that had first drawn him in: so wide, so blue, like the sea all around them and the vast Hawaiian sky above. And she had looked up at him with her wet hair plastered to her head and her sensual lips parted, as if he were all the world. He had felt the same.

How times changed.

It was not enough that he had lost his life-long, renowned control with her then. That he had betrayed his family's wishes and his own expectations and married a nobody from a place about as far away from his beloved northern Italy as it was possible to get. He had been supposed to choose an appropriately titled bride, a woman of endless pedigree and celebrated blood—a fate that he had accepted as simply one more aspect of the many duties that comprised his title. He was the *Principe di Felici*. His family's roots extended back into thirteenth-century Florence. He had expected his future wife to have a heritage no less impressive.

Yet he had eloped with Bethany instead. He had married her because, for the first and only time in his life, he had felt wild and reckless. Passionate. Alive. He had not been able to imagine returning to his life without her.

And he had paid for his folly ever since.

Leo turned from the window, and set his empty tumbler down on the wide glass table before him. He raked his fingers through his hair and refused to speculate as to the meaning of the heaviness in his chest. He did not spare a glance for the sumptuous leather couches, nor the intricate statuary that accented the great room.

He thought only of Bethany, saw only Bethany, a haunting he had come to regard as commonplace over the years. She was his one regret, his one mistake. His wife.

He had already compromised more than he could have ever imagined possible, against all advice and all instinct. He had assumed her increasing sullenness in their first year of marriage was merely a phase she had been going through—a necessary shift from her quiet life into his far more colorful one—and had therefore allowed her more leeway than he should have.

He had suffered her temper, her baffling re-

sistance to performing her official duties, even
her horror that he had wanted to start a family
so quickly. He had foolishly believed that she
needed time to grow into her role as his wife,
when retrospect made it clear that what she'd
truly needed was a firmer hand.

He had let her leave him, shocked and hurt
in ways he'd refused to acknowledge that she
would attempt it in the first place. He had assumed she would come to her senses while
they were apart, that she needed time to adjust
to the idea of her new responsibilities and the
pressures of her new role and title. Neither was
something a common, simple girl from Toronto
could have been prepared for, he had come to
understand.

After all, he had spent his whole life coming
to terms with the weight and heft of the Di
Marco heritage and its many demands upon
him. He had reluctantly let her have her freedom—after all, she had been so young when
they had married. So unformed. So unsophis-
ticated.

And this was how she repaid him. Lies about
a lover, when she should have known that he
had her every movement tracked and would
certainly have allowed no lover to further sully
his name. Claims that she wished to divorce
him, unforgivably uttered in public where

anyone might hear. Aspersions cast without trepidation upon his character, his honor.

He took a kind of solace in the anger that surged through him. It was far, far easier to be angry than to confront what he knew lay beneath. And he had vowed that he would never show her his vulnerabilities—never again.

Revenge would be sweet, he decided, and he would have no qualms whatsoever in extracting it. He thought then of that confusing vulnerability he'd thought he'd seen but dismissed it.

Di Marcos did not divorce. Ever.

The Princess Di Marco, Principessa di Felici, had two duties: to support her husband in all he did, and to bear him heirs to secure the title. Leo sank down onto the nearest couch and blew out a breath.

It was about time that Bethany started living up to her responsibilities.

And, if those responsibilities forced her to return to him as she should have done years before, all the better.

Bethany should not have been surprised when she looked up from packing a box the next morning to see Leo looming in the doorway of her bedroom. But she could not contain the gasp that escaped her.

She jerked back and pressed her hand against

her wildly thumping heart. It was surprise, she told herself; no more than surprise. Certainly not that wild, desperate hope she refused to acknowledge within her.

"What are you doing here?" she asked, appalled at the breathiness of her voice. And, in any case, she knew what he was doing: this was his house, wasn't it? Three stories of stately brick and pedigreed old-money in Rosedale, Toronto's wealthiest neighborhood. It was exactly where Prince Leopoldo Di Marco, *Principe di Felici*, ought to reside.

Bethany hated it—she hated everything the house stood for. Her occupying such a monied, ancestrally pre-determined sort of space seemed like a contradiction in terms—like one more lie. Yet Leo had insisted that she live in this house, or in Italy with him, and three years ago she had not had the strength to choose her own third option.

As long as she lived under this roof, she was essentially consenting to her sham of a marriage—and Leo's control. Yet she had stayed here anyway, until she could no longer pretend that she was not on some level waiting for him to come and claim her.

Once she had accepted that depressing truth, she had known she had no choice but to act.

"Surely my presence cannot be quite so

shocking?" Leo asked in that way of his that felt like a slap, as if she was too foolish, too naïve. It set her teeth on edge.

"Are you so grand that you cannot ring the doorbell like anyone else?" she asked more fiercely than she'd intended.

It did not help that she had not slept well, her mind racing and her skin buzzing as if she'd been wildly over-caffeinated. Nor did it help that she had dressed to pack boxes today, in a pair of faded blue jeans and a simple, blue long-sleeved T-shirt, with her curls tied up in a haphazard knot on the back of her head. Not exactly the height of elegance.

Leo, of course, looked exquisite and impeccable in a charcoal-colored buttoned-down shirt that clung to his flat, hard chest and a pair of dark, wool trousers that only emphasized the strong lines of his body.

He leaned against the doorjamb and watched her for a simmering moment, his mouth unsmiling, those coffee eyes hooded.

"Is your lot in life truly so egregious, Bethany?" he asked softly. "Do I deserve quite this level of hostility?"

Something thicker than regret—and much too close to shame—turned over in her stomach. But Bethany forced herself not to do what every instinct screamed at her to do: she would not apologize, cajole or soothe. She knew from painful experience that there was only one way such things would end. Leo took and took until there was nothing in her left to give.

So she did not cross to him. She did not even shrug an apology. She only brushed a fallen strand of hair away from her face, ignored the spreading hollowness within and concentrated on the box in front of her on the wide bed.

"I realize this is your house," she said stiffly into the uncomfortable silence. "But I would appreciate it if you would do me the courtesy of announcing your arrival, rather than appearing in doorways. It seems only polite."

There were so many land mines littered about the floor and so many memories cluttering the air between them—too many. Her chest felt tight, yet all she could think of was her first night in Italy and Leo's patient instructions about how she would be expected to behave— delivered between kisses in his grand bed. He had grown less patient and much less affectionate over time, when it had become clear to all involved that he had made a dreadful mistake in marrying someone like Bethany. Her mouth tightened at the memory.

"Of course," Leo murmured. His dark gaze tracked her movements. "You are already packing your belongings?"

"Don't worry," she said, shooting him a look. "I won't take anything that isn't mine."

That muscle in his jaw jumped and his eyes narrowed.

"I am relieved to hear it," he said after a thick, simmering moment.

When she had folded the same white cotton sweater four times, and still failed to do it correctly, Bethany gave up. She turned from the bed and faced him, swallowing back any fear, anxiety or any of the softer, deeper things she pretended not to feel—because none would do her any good.

"Leo, really." She shoved her hands into her hip pockets so he could not see that they were curling into fists. "Why are you here?"

"I have not visited this place in a long time," he said, and she hated him for it.

"No," she agreed, her voice a rasp in the sudden tense air of the room.

How dared he refer to that night—that awful, shameful night? How could she have behaved that way, so out of control and crazed with her heartbreak, her desperate resolve to really, truly leave him? And how could all of that fury and fire have twisted around and around and left her so wanton, so shameless, that she could have...*mated* with him like that? With such ferocity it still made her shiver years later.

She'd had no idea of the depths to which she could sink. Not until he'd taken her there and then left her behind to stew in it.

"I have news," he said, his gaze moving over her face, once again making her wonder exactly what he could read there. "But I do not think you will be pleased." He straightened from the door and suddenly seemed much closer than he should. She fought to stand still, to keep from backing away.

"Well?" she asked.

But he did not answer her immediately. Instead, he moved into the room, seeming to take it over, somehow, seeming to diminish it with the force of his presence.

Bethany felt the way his eyes raked over the white linen piled high on the unmade bed even as her memory played back too-vivid recollections of the night she most wanted to forget. The crash and splintering of a vase against the wall. Her fists against his chest. His fierce, mocking laughter. His shirt torn from him with her own desperate hands. His mouth fused to hers. His hands like fire, punishment and glory all over her, lifting her, spurring her on, damning them both.

She shook it off and found him watching her, a gleam in his dark gaze, as if he too remembered the very same scenes. He stood at the foot of the bed, too close to her. He could too easily reach over and tip her onto the mattress, and Bethany was not at all certain what might happen then.

She froze, appalled at the direction of her thoughts. A familiar despair washed through her, all the more bitter because she knew it so well. Still she wanted him. Still. She did not understand how that could be true. She did not want to understand; she only wanted it—and him—to go away. She wanted to be free of the heavy weight of him, of his loss. She simply wanted to be free.

It was as if he could read her mind. The silence between them seemed charged, alive. His gaze dropped from hers to flick over her mouth then lower, to test her curves, and she could feel it as clearly as if he'd put his hands upon her.

"You said you had something to tell me," she managed to grate out as if her thighs did not feel loose, ready, despite her feelings of hopelessness. As if her core did not pulse for him. As if she did not feel that electricity skate over her skin, letting her know he was near, stirring up that excitement she would give anything to deny.

"I do," Leo murmured, dark and tall, too big and too powerful to be in this room. This house. Her life. "The divorce. There is a complication."

"What complication?" she asked, suspicious, though her traitorous body did not seem to care. It throbbed for him, hot and needy.

"I am afraid that it cannot be done remotely." He shrugged in that supremely Italian way, as if to say that the vagaries of such things were beyond anyone's control, even his.

"You cannot mean…?" she began. His gaze found hers then, so very dark and commanding, and she felt goosebumps rise along her arms and neck. It was as though someone walked across her grave, she thought distantly.

"There is no getting around it," he said, but his voice was not apologetic. His gaze was direct. And Bethany went completely cold. "I am afraid that you must return to Italy."

CHAPTER THREE

"I AM not going back to Italy," Bethany blurted out, shocked that he would suggest such an outlandish thing.

Had he lost his mind? He had managed to ruin the entire country for her. She couldn't imagine what would ever induce her to return to it. In her mind, any return to Italy meant a return to the spineless creature she had been when she lived there; she could not—would not—be that person ever again.

But Leo merely watched her with those knowing, mocking eyes as if he knew something she did not.

"Don't be ridiculous!" she tossed at him to offset the panic skipping through her nerves.

Leo's dark brows rose in a haughty sort of amazement, and she remembered belatedly that the *Principe di Felici* was not often called things like 'ridiculous.' He was no doubt more used to being showered in honorifics. 'Your

Excellency.' 'My Prince.' She bit her lower lip but did not retract her words.

"I am afraid there is no other way, if you wish to divorce me," he said. If he were another man, she might have thought that tone apologetic. But this was Leo, and his eyes were too unreadable, so she could only be suspicious. "If you wish to remain merely separated, of course, you can continue to do as you please."

"I am not the idiot you seem to think," she said, her mind reeling. "I am a Canadian citizen. I do not need to go all the way to Italy to divorce you—I can do it right here."

"That would be true, had you not signed all the papers," Leo said calmly. His gaze was disconcertingly direct, seeming to push inside of her and render her transparent. Yet she could not seem to look away. His head tilted slightly to one side. "When you first arrived at the castello. Perhaps you do not recall."

"Of course I remember." Bethany let out a short laugh even as her stomach twisted anxiously. "How could anyone forget three days of legal documents?"

She remembered all too well the intimidating sheaves of paper that had been thrust at her by an unsmiling phalanx of attorneys, her signature required again and again. Sign here, principessa.

Most of the documents had been in Italian, affixed with serious and official seals and covered with intimidatingly dense prose. She had not understood a single thing that had been put in front of her, but she had been so desperately in love with her brand-new husband that she had signed everything anyway.

That great cavern of sorrow she carried within her yawned open, but she ignored it. She could not collapse in that way. Not now.

"Then you perhaps have forgotten what, exactly, it is that you signed," Leo continued, his cool, faintly mocking voice kindling fear and fury in equal measure and sending both shooting along Bethany's limbs like a hot wind.

"I have no idea what I signed," she was forced to admit. It pained her that she could ever have been so blindly trusting, even five years ago at the start of her marriage when she had thought Leo Di Marco was the whole of the cosmos.

He inclined his head toward her, as if that statement said all that need be said.

"I signed it because you told me to sign it," Bethany said quietly. "I assumed you were concerned with my best interests as well as your own." She eyed him and gathered her courage around her like a shield. "Not a mistake I intend to repeat."

"Of course not," Leo said in that smooth, sardonic tone, crossing his arms over his hard chest.

He looked around the room, pointedly taking in the elegance of the furnishings, the pale blue walls beneath delicate moldings and the thick, rich carpeting beneath their feet.

"Because," he continued in that same tone, "as we have established, you have lived as if in a nightmare ever since the day you agreed to marry me."

"Are you going to tell me what rights I signed away, or would you prefer to stand there making sarcastic remarks?" Bethany snapped at him, exasperated at her own distressing softening as well as his patronizing tone. She hated the way he looked at her then, his arrogant gaze growing somehow more intimidating, burning into her.

"My apologies," he said, his tone scathing. "I was unaware that my preferences were of any interest to you."

He almost smiled then, a hard, edgy crook of his sensual mouth. Bethany wanted to look away but found she couldn't—she was as trapped, as if he held her in his hands, which she knew would be the end of her.

"But that is neither here nor there, is it?" he asked in that deadly, soft tone that sent shivers down Bethany's spine and twisted through her stomach. "The salient point is that you agreed that any divorce proceedings, should they ever become necessary, would be held in an Italian court under Italian law."

"And, naturally, I have only your word for that," Bethany pointed out, horrified that her voice sounded so insubstantial. She cleared her throat and jerked her gaze from his as if she might turn to stone were she to lose herself any further in that bittersweet darkness. "I could have agreed to anything and I would have no way of knowing, would I?"

"If you wish to hire a translator and have the documents examined, I will instruct my secretaries to begin compiling copies for your review immediately," Leo said in a mild way, yet with that sardonic current beneath.

"And how long will that take?" Bethany asked, her bitterness swelling, hinting at the great wealth of tears beneath. She blinked them back. "Years? This is all just a game to you, isn't it?"

His gaze seemed to ignite then, hard, hot and furious. The room constricted around them, narrowing, until there was nothing but Leo—the real Leo, she thought wildly—too dark, too angry and too close. Bethany felt panic race through her; a surge of adrenaline and something far more dangerous kicked up her pulse, hardened her nipples and pooled between her legs. She hated herself for that betrayal above all else.

And she suddenly realized how close together they were standing, with only the corner of the platform bed between them. She could reach out her hand and lay it against his hard pectoral muscles, or the fascinating valley between them. She could inhale his scent.

She could completely ruin herself and all she'd fought so hard to achieve!

"You must return to Italy if you wish to divorce me," he said, his voice low and furious, like a dark electrical current that set her alight. "There is no other option available to you."

"How convenient for you," she managed to say somehow, not fighting the faint trembling that shook her—not certain she could have hid it if she'd tried. "I wonder how the foreign wife of an Italian prince can expect to be treated in Italy?"

"It is not your foreign birth that should worry you, Bethany," Leo said, his noble features so arrogant, so coldly and impossibly beautiful, even now—his low voice like a dark melody. "The abandonment of your husband and subsequent taking of a lover? That, I am afraid, may force the courts to find you at fault for the dissolution of the marriage." He shrugged, seemingly nonchalant, though his eyes were far too dark, far too hard. "But you are quite proud of both those things, are you not? Why should it distress you?"

Bethany felt as if something huge and heavy was crushing her, making it impossible to breathe, making tears prick at the backs of her eyes when she had no desire to weep. It was the way he said 'abandonment' and 'lover,' perhaps. It tore at her. It made her nearly confess the truth to him, confess her lie, simply to see his gaze warm. It made her wish she could still believe in dreams she had been forced to grow out of years ago.

But she knew better than to give him ammunition. Better he should hate her and release her than think well of her and keep her tied to him in this half-life, no matter how much it hurt her.

"There must be another way," she said after a moment or two, battling to keep her voice even.

Leo merely shook his head, his features carefully blank once again, just that polite exterior masking all the anger and arrogance she knew filled him from within. She could feel it all around them, tightening like a vice. Too much emotion. Too much history.

"I don't accept that," Bethany said, frowning at him.

"There are many things that you do not accept, it seems," Leo said silkily. "But that does not make them any less true."

He wanted her. He always wanted her. He had stopped asking himself why that should be.

He did not care about her lies, her insults—or he did not care enough, now, having been without her for so long. He only wanted to be deep inside of her, her legs wrapped around his waist, where there could be only the truth of that hot, silken connection. The only truth that had ever mattered, no matter what she chose to believe. No matter what he felt.

She should know better than to row with him so close to a bed. She should remember that all her posturing, all her demands, rages and pouts, disappeared the moment he touched her. His hands itched to prove that to her.

She pushed her curls back from her face and looked unutterably tired for a flashing moment. "I would ask you what you mean, and I am certain you would love to tell me, but I am tired of your games, Leo," she said in that quiet yet matter-of-fact voice that he was growing to dislike intensely. "I will not go back to Italy. Ever."

He thought of the vulnerability he had sensed in her, that undercurrent of pain. He could see hints of it in the way she looked at him now, the careful way she held herself. Sex and temper, he understood; both could be solved in the same way. But this was something else.

A game, he assured himself. This is just another game.

"You make such grand proclamations, luce mio," he said softly, never taking his eyes from hers. "How can you keep them all straight? Today you will not go to Italy. Three years ago you would not remain my wife. So many threats, Bethany, all of which end in nothing."

"Those are not threats," she threw at him, her eyes dark in that way that made things shift uncomfortably in him, her soft mouth trembling. "They are the unvarnished truth. I'm sorry if you are not used to hearing such a thing, but then you surround yourself with sycophants, don't you? You have only yourself to blame."

Leo moved toward her, his gaze tight on hers. "There were so many sweeping threats, as I recall," he said softly, mockingly, as if she had not spoken. As if there were no shifts, no darkness, no depths he could not comprehend. "You would not speak to me again once you left Italy. You would not remain in this house even twenty-four hours after I left you here. They begin to run together, do they not?"

She only stared at him, her blue eyes wide, furious and something else, something deeper. But her very presence before him, in the house she had vowed to leave, was all the answer that was needed.

"And we cannot forget my favorite threat of all, can we?" He closed the space between them then, though he did not reach over and touch her as he longed to do. He was so close she was forced to tilt her face up toward his if she wanted to look at him. Her lips parted slightly, her eyes widening as heat bloomed on her cheeks.

"Is this supposed to terrify me?" she asked, but it was hardly a whisper, barely a thread of sound. "Am I expected to cower away from you in fear and awe?"

"You promised me you would never go near me again, that I disgusted you," he said softly, looking down into her eyes, reading one emotion after another—none of them disgust. "Is that why you shake, Bethany? Is this disgust?"

"It is nothing so deep as disgust," she said, her voice a thread of sound, her eyes too bright. She cleared her throat. "It is simply acute boredom with this situation."

"You are a liar, then and now," he said, reluctantly intrigued by the shadows that chased through her bright blue eyes. He was not surprised when she moved away from him, putting more space between their bodies as if that might dampen the heat they generated between them. As if anything ever could.

"That is almost funny, Leo," she said in a quiet voice, her gaze dark. "Coming from you."

"Tell me, Bethany, how have I deceived you?" he asked softly, watching her school her expressive face into the smooth blandness he hated. "What are my crimes?"

"I refuse to discuss this with you, as if you do not already know," she said, squaring her shoulders. "As if we have not gone over it again and again to the point of nausea."

"Very well, then," he said, hearing that harsh edge in his voice, unable to control it. "Then let us discuss your crimes. We can start with your lover."

His words seemed to hang there, accusation and curse wrapping around her like a vise. She wanted to scream, to rage, to shove at him. To collapse to the floor and sob out her anguish.

But she could not bring herself to move. She felt pinned as much by the heat in his dark gaze as her own eternal folly. Why had she told him such an absurd lie? Why had she put herself in a position where he could claim the moral high-ground over her?

"You do not wish to discuss my lover," she told him stiffly, hating herself, her own voice sounding like a stranger's. But she had to make it believable, didn't she? "You do not compare well in any department."

"How will you tell him that you cannot ever do more than commit adultery so long as you remain married to me?" he murmured in that way of his that seemed to channel directly along her spine, making her feel shivery and weak. "What man would tolerate such a thing, when all you need do is fly to Italy to take care of that one, small detail?"

"He is enormously tolerant," Bethany said through her teeth. The word 'adultery' seemed to ricochet through her, chipping off pieces of her heart until they fell like stones into the pit of her stomach.

"As it happens," Leo said in that quiet, lethal tone, "I am flying to Italy tomorrow morning. We could finish with this unpleasantness in no time at all."

It paralyzed her. For a moment, she simply stared at him, lost, as if he'd reached over and torn her heart from her chest. It was as if she could no longer feel it beating. She could not begin to imagine the damage his capitulation caused her. She did not want to imagine it.

"If there is no other way," she said slowly, feeling as if she was teetering on the edge of a vast, deep abyss, as if her voice was something she'd dug up somewhere, rusty and unused, not hers at all. "Then I suppose I will have to go to Italy."

Leo's eyes darkened with that pure male fire she knew too well. It called to that twisted part of her, the part she most wanted to deny.

Because despite the pain, the grief and the loneliness, she still wanted him. She still ached for him, that wave of longing and lust that made everything else the very lies he accused her of telling. His body. His presence. The light of his smile, the brush of his hand, the very fact of his nearness. She ached.

Time seemed to stand still. There was only that fierce, knowing gleam in his eyes, as there had always been. One touch, his gaze promised her, hot, gleaming and sure. Only one small touch and she would be his. Only that, and she would betray herself completely.

And she knew some part of her wanted him to do it—wanted him to tumble her to the bed and take her with all the easy command and consummate skill that had always shaken her so completely, melted her so fully, made her his in every way. She no longer even bothered to despair of herself.

"My plane awaits," he said softly, and she could hear the intense satisfaction behind his words. As if he had known they would end up in exactly this place. As if he had made it so. As if he could read her mind.

"I will not travel with you," she told him, holding her head high even as she surrendered, because she could not think of anything else to do, any way to escape this. Escape him. Their past. She would go to Italy and fight it there, where it had gone so wrong in the first place.

She glared at him. "I will find my own way there."

And Leo, damn him, smiled.

CHAPTER FOUR

THE small, achingly picturesque village of Felici—ancestral seat of the Di Marco family and the very last place Bethany ever wanted to visit again—clung to the hillside in the late-afternoon sun, red-roofed and white-walled.

The local church thrust its proud white steeple high into the air, bells tolling out the turn of the hour. Carefully cultivated vineyards stretched out across the tidy Felici Valley, reaching toward the alpine foothills rising in the distance. And at the highest point in the village loomed the ancient Castello di Felici itself, defining the very hill it clung to, announcing the might and power of the Di Marco family to all who ventured near.

Yet all Bethany could see was ghosts.

She drove the hired car along the main road that wound up into the village, so renowned for its narrow medieval streets and prosperous, cheerful architecture. She pulled into the small parking area near the pensione located at the hill's midway point. But she still couldn't seem to draw a full breath, or calm the nervous fluttering in her belly.

It had been that way since her plane had taken off from Toronto two nights before. She had only managed a fitful, restless kind of doze for most of the long overnight flight. When she had managed to sleep, her dreams had been filled with dread, loss and panic and Leo's bittersweet, chocolate gaze like a laser cutting through her. Hardly rejuvenating.

"My men will meet you at the airport," he had told her, in that peremptory manner that made it clear there was to be no discussion before taking his leave from the house in Rosedale.

It had been like a flashback into the very heart of their married life, and not a pleasant one. Bethany had not been able to stand the thought of doing what he'd decreed she should do, and not simply because he'd decreed it. She'd felt claustrophobic imagining how it would go: she would be marched from the plane, deposited into one of the endless fleet of gleaming black cars he had at his disposal and spirited away to his castello like…property.

She shuddered anew, just thinking of it. That

was exactly why she had opted to fly into Rome instead of the much-closer Milan.

She'd fought off her exhaustion throughout the long drive up the middle of the country, arriving in the outskirts of Milan early the previous evening. She'd fallen gratefully into a clean bed in a cheap hotel outside the city limits and had finally slept. It had been nearly noon when she'd pulled herself out of bed, cotton-headed and reeling, her thudding heart telling her the anxiety dreams had continued even if she hadn't quite remembered them once awake.

She'd remembered other things, however, no matter how she'd tried to keep the memories at bay.

"Ah, luce mio, how I love you," he had whispered as he had held her close, high on a balcony that overlooked the Felici Valley as the sun had set before them that first night in Italy.

My light, she had thought, dazed by him as if he were all the fire and song of the stars above. "Why am I your light?" she had asked. She'd meant, how can you love me when you are you and I am me?

"These eyes," he had murmured, kissing one closed lid and then the next. "They are as blue as the summer sky. How could you be anything but light, with eyes such as these?"

She had lingered over strong espresso in a

café near her hotel after she woke, putting off the inevitable for as long as she could. With every bone in her body, every fiber of her being, she had not wanted to make the last leg of this journey. She had not wanted to travel the last few hours into the countryside, further and further into the past. Further and further into everything she'd wanted so badly and lost despite herself.

It seemed impossible that any of this was really happening. It reminded her of the dreams she'd had on and off since leaving Italy three years ago. She would dream that she had never left at all, that she had only imagined it, that she was still trying to bite her tongue and keep her feelings to herself like the dutiful principessa she had failed to become and that the hard, lonely years since leaving Leo had been the dream.

She had always woken in a panic, her face wet with tears, the bedroom seeming to echo around her as if she had screamed out in her sleep.

There was no waking up from this, Bethany thought now, feeling flushed, too hot with emotions she refused to examine. She stared at the ivy-covered wall before her as if it could help her—as if anything could.

She climbed out of the car and couldn't help

the deep breath she took then, almost against her will. The air was crisp, clean, and sweet-smelling. She fancied she could smell the Italian sun as it headed west high above her; she could see the Alps in the far distance, the vines and the olive groves. She could smell cheerful local meals spicing the early-evening air: rich polenta and creamy, decadent risotto, the mellow undertone of warming olive oil on the breeze.

It brought back too many memories. It hurt.

She was unable to keep herself from a brooding look up at the castello itself. It sat there, the high walls seeming to be part of the cliff itself, feudal and imposing, crouched over the town like a dragon guarding its treasure. She could easily imagine generations of Di Marcos fighting off sieges, bolstering their wealth and influence from the safety of those towering heights. She almost imagined she could see Leo, like some feudal lord high on the walls, the world at his feet.

Bethany almost wished she could hate the place, for on some level she blamed the stones themselves for destroying her marriage. It was a visceral feeling, all guts and irrationality, but the girl who had walked inside those walls had never walked out again.

She wished she could hate the thick, stone

walls, the now-unused battlements. She wished she could hate the drawbridge that led through the outer walls of what had originally been a monastery, over the defunct moat and beneath the Di Marco coat of arms that had first been emblazoned above the entryway in the fifteenth century.

"It is so beautiful!" she had breathed, overcome as she'd walked through the great stone archway at the top of the drawbridge. He had swept her into his arms, spinning them both around in a circle until they had both laughed with the sheer joy of it right there in the grand hall.

"Not so beautiful as you," he had said, his gaze serious, though his mouth had curved into a smile she'd been able to feel inside her own chest. "Never so beautiful as you, amore mio."

Shaking the memory off, annoyed by her own melancholy, Bethany pulled her suitcase from the passenger seat and headed toward the entrance of the pensione. She had chosen this place deliberately: it was brand new. There would be much less chance of an awkward run-in with anyone she might have known three years ago.

She was reasonably confident she could avoid Leo as easily.

"It should not require more than two weeks

of your time," Leo had estimated with a careless shrug. Two weeks, perhaps a bit more. She had survived the last three years, she'd thought, so what were a few more weeks?

But she couldn't help the feelings that dragged at her, pulling her inexorably toward that vast cavern of loneliness and pain inside that she could not allow to claim her any longer.

Just as she couldn't help one last, doubtful look at the castello over her shoulder as she pushed open the door to the lobby and walked inside.

"I am so sorry," the man said from behind the counter in heavily accented English. "The room—it is not yet ready."

But Bethany knew the truth. She could see it in the man's averted gaze, the welcoming smile that had dropped from his lips. It had happened the moment she'd said her name. It did not seem to matter that she'd used her maiden name, as she'd grown used to doing in Toronto.

Her hands tightened around the handle of her suitcase, so hard her knuckles whitened, but she managed to curve her lips into an approximation of a polite smile.

"How odd," she murmured past the tightness in her throat. "I was certain the check-in time was three o'clock, and it is already past five."

"If you would not mind waiting…" The man smiled helplessly and gestured toward the small seating-area at the far side of the small lobby.

Feeling helpless, Bethany turned from the counter, aware that her eyes were filled with a dangerous heat. She walked across the lobby with careful precision and then sat on the plush sofa, feeling as if she was made of glass, fragile and precarious. And then feeling broken, somehow, when the man picked up the telephone and murmured something she could not quite hear in rapid Italian.

Sure enough, not ten minutes later the front door was pulled open and two men in dark suits entered. Bethany did not recognize them personally, but she had no doubt at all about who they were.

They walked toward her, coming to a stop only a foot or two away. She stared straight ahead, willing herself to stay calm, adult, and rational, as she'd been so sure she'd remain. She fought to maintain her composure, though her stomach twisted and her heart beat too hard against her ribs.

"Principessa," the larger of the two men murmured in tones of the greatest respect— which made Bethany that much more furious, somehow, and that much more despairing. "Per favore…?"

What could she do? This was Leo's village. He was its prince. She had been a fool to think he would let her return to it without controlling her every move. Back when she had felt more charitable toward him she'd told herself he simply knew no other way to behave, that he had been raised to be this dictatorial, that it was not his fault.

Today, she knew the truth. This was who he was. This was who he wanted to be. What she wanted had never mattered, and never, ever would.

So she simply rose to her feet with as much dignity and grace as she could muster. She let Leo's men guide her to the expected gleaming black sedan that waited outside, elegant and imprisoning, and climbed obediently into the back seat.

And then she sat there, furious, helpless and as brokenhearted as the day she'd left, as they drove her straight into the jaws of the castello.

It was all exactly as she remembered, exactly as she still dreamed.

The great castello was quiet around her—it was open to the public only on certain days of the week or by appointment—and felt empty, even though she knew that hordes of servants were all around her, perhaps even watching her, just out of sight.

Bethany felt a drowning sensation, as if she was being sucked backward in time, thrown back four years into that other life where she had been so miserable, so terribly alone. And it had been worse because she had not known how alone she was at first—she had still believed that she would recover from her father's death with Leo's help, that he would become the family she so deeply craved.

Instead, he had abandoned her in every way that mattered.

As if the stones themselves remembered that grief, that ache, they seemed to echo not just her footsteps as she walked but her memories of those awful days here when she'd been so isolated, scared and abandoned.

She barely saw the impressive entryway, the tapestries along the stone walls inside the grand entrance, the rooms filled with priceless art and antiques, each item resplendent with its pedigree, its heritage, its worth across centuries. Her silent escorts ushered her up above the public rooms to the family wing, then down the long, gleaming hallway toward her old, familiar door. But all she could see was the past.

And then it was done. Her suitcase was deposited just inside her chamber and the door was closed behind her with a muted click. She stood inside the bedroom suite that had once been hers, her luxurious cage, quite as if she had never left.

Bethany let her head drop slightly forward, squeezing shut her eyes as she stood there in the center of the grand room. This was the principessa's historic suite, handed down over the ages from one wife to the next. It boasted the finest furnishings, gilt-edged and ornate. The bed was canopied in gold, the regal bedspread an opulent shade of red. Everything was made of the darkest, richest wood, lovingly crafted and polished to a high shine. There was never a hint of dust in this room, never an item out of place—except for Bethany herself, she thought wryly.

She did not have to investigate to know that all was precisely as it had been the last time she'd been here. She did not have to walk to the towering windows to know what she would see through them: the finely sculpted gardens and beyond them, the rooftops of the village and the gentle, inviting roll of Italian countryside reaching for the horizon. All of it was beautiful beyond measure, and yet somehow capable of making that ache inside of her grow so much more acute.

And she did not have to turn when she heard

the paneled side-door open because she knew exactly who would be standing there. But she could not seem to help herself, her gaze was drawn to him as if he were a flickering flame and she no more than a moth. She wished even that did not hurt her, but it did. It still did.

Leo lounged against the paneled door frame, his long, lean form packed into dark trousers and a cashmere black sweater that emphasized his whipcord strength. His eyes seemed nearly black, and she fought off the urge to rub at the back of her neck where the fine hairs there whispered in warning.

He looked dark and powerful, like one of the ancient Roman gods that had once roamed this land, capricious and cruel. And she knew he was bent on vengeance just the same. He did not show her that sardonic smile of his, that mocking twist of his sensual lips.

He did not need to. Her very presence was enough.

Already she felt as if she'd lost everything. Again.

"Ah, principessa," Leo said, his tone laced with irony. "Welcome home."

He took a moment to drink in the sight of her, back where she belonged after all of this time. Finally.

It almost eased the three years' worth of simmering anger and the deeper current beneath it he felt when he looked at her. She crossed her arms over her middle, as if it hurt her to stand there in the ancestral bedroom where she had once lived. Where—he knew, whether she did or not—she would live again.

He would allow for no other outcome.

She looked tired, he thought, eyeing her critically. She was unusually pale, though her head was high with the same kind of quiet pride she had showed in Toronto. He did not want her pride, he thought; he wanted her passion. And then her acquiescence.

Because he could think of no other way to reach her. And he had exhausted his futile attempts to pretend that that was not exactly what he wanted.

She wore a tight white T-shirt that clung to her pert, full breasts and a sweater wrap that hung down to her thighs in a soft blue that made her eyes glow even brighter than usual. She still wore those faded denim jeans. In some kind of deliberate rebellion, he had no doubt, though the triumph he felt that he had managed to bring her home far outweighed any disapproval he might have felt about her choice of wardrobe.

He wanted to touch her, taste her. Trace the

shape of her graceful neck, sink his fingers into her dark curls. Welcome her back to her home, her responsibilities, him, in the way they would both find most pleasurable. In the only way he knew would bind her to him without having to touch on all that seemed to threaten from beneath the certainty of the fire that raged between them.

If he could only have that fire again, he thought, he would know better how to tend it. He would not let it go again so easily.

The vast room seemed smaller suddenly and her eyes widened with awareness. He smiled slightly. Bethany looked away and swallowed. Leo let his gaze trace the fine column of her throat and saw the wash of red that began to climb there.

"I do not understand why I was dragged from the inn of my choice," she said after a moment.

"I see you are starting at once on the offensive," he murmured, mildly reproving. "Are you not tired of it yet? I feel certain we have enough to discuss without any unnecessary histrionics."

Her brows rose in astonishment. "There is no reason for me to stay here. It is hardly histrionic to say so." Her voice was matter-of-fact, and rubbed him entirely up the wrong way.

"Why?" he asked coolly. "Other than the fact

you'd made your usual dramatic proclamations about how you would never return, what objection can you possibly have to staying in the castello?"

She stared at him with a curious expression that Leo had never seen before—one that suggested that he was not very bright. It made him feel…restless. A slow beat of that same old anger and a very familiar frustration began to hammer in his gut, mixed with a new edge that had everything to do with the calm, cool way she looked at him. As if he was the person outside the bounds of propriety and self-control when that had always been her role.

"I do not want to be here." She said it very deliberately, her gaze still on his in that insulting manner. "I need no other objection than that."

Leo straightened from the doorway, coldly amused at the way she jerked back, as if she expected him to lunge at her. He wished he could. He wished he could simply throw her over his shoulder and take her down with him to the soft mattress of the bed behind her. But he knew that, as delightful as it would be to lose himself in her body, it would only delay the inevitable.

Sex had never been their problem. It had been a weapon, a hiding place, a muddying of already murky waters. He knew with a sudden, devastating insight into the part of himself he preferred to ignore that he could not let it be used as such any longer.

He wanted her back where she belonged, and this time he would have all of her.

"Let me be clear," he said, his voice clipped. Authoritative. "You will not stay in the village. The fact that you attempted to do so after the childish stunt you pulled with your flight— without my ring on your finger or my name, though you are easily identifiable and must know the shame that casts upon this house— only underscores your selfishness."

He watched that red flush on her skin deepen one shade darker, then two. Her soft mouth firmed into a hard line he found unaccountably fascinating.

"How incredibly patronizing you are, Leo," she said coolly, though he could hear temper and something else crackling through her voice. "Patronizing and dismissive."

Leo shrugged. "If you feel you must call me names because it is difficult for you to accept that you have returned here, I will not blame you," he said.

Whatever it took, she would truly be his wife again, he vowed. She would be the principessa he had imagined she could be. He would not allow for any other outcome. Not this time.

Her blue eyes blazed into hard sapphires.

"I am having no difficulty at all accepting that I am here," she bit out. "I am, however, unable to process the fact that you feel comfortable speaking to me as if I am a child."

"I am well aware that you are not a child," he said. His gaze met hers and held. "It has always been your behavior that causes the confusion."

Her eyes narrowed. He could sense her temper skyrocketing, but could not imagine what it was that so enraged her. The simple truth? He was surprised she had not already thrown something at him, or launched her own body at his, nails like claws, as she would have done in the past.

He watched, fascinated despite himself, as she visibly fought for control. This was not the Bethany he knew. His Bethany was a creature of passion and regret, rages and tears. She threw precious china against the wall, screamed herself hoarse, threw tantrums that shook the ancient stones beneath their feet. She was not capable of reining in her temper once it ignited, like the woman before him.

He could see it in her eyes, the rage and the passion, the fury and the heat. But she did not move to strike him. She did not scream like a banshee. She only faced him.

He did not know if he admired her unexpected fortitude, or felt it as a loss.

"I will not be spoken to as if I am a recalcitrant adolescent or a lowly member of your staff, Leo," she told him, her voice tight and hard. "I understand that you live in a world where you need only express a desire and it is met, but I am not your underling. I am a grown woman. I do, in fact, know my own mind."

Leo let out a short laugh. "I am delighted to hear it," he said. "Does that mean the antique vases are safe from your rampages? I will notify the household staff."

Her face darkened, but she did not scream at him. Against his will, Leo's fascination deepened.

"Treat me like a child and I will treat you exactly the same way," she said instead, her words very precise, very pointed. "And I very much doubt your exalted sense of self could handle it."

She was an adult? She had outgrown her childishness? He was thrilled, he told himself, eyeing her narrowly. Overjoyed, in fact. Wasn't that why he'd allowed her to run off to Canada in the first place? She had been so very young when he had met her; far younger than her years. Hadn't he wanted her to mature?

He had only himself to blame if he did not quite care for the specific direction her show of maturity had taken—if he found he preferred the angry child to this unknowable woman who stood before him with unreadable eyes.

"You are still my wife," he said after a long moment, his tone even. "As long as that is true, you cannot stay in the village. It will cause too much comment."

"Thank you for speaking to me as an adult for once," she said. Her chin tilted up and her bright eyes sparkled with a combination of defiance and a certain resignation that made his hackles rise. "What does that say about you, I wonder, that it was so hard to do?"

CHAPTER FIVE

"I TRUST that was rhetorical," he said mildly enough.

But Leo's gaze was too sharp, and Bethany knew that she could no longer maintain any pretense of calm if she continued to look at him.

She moved, restless and more agitated than she wanted to admit, wandering further into the room. She let her gaze dance over the painting that dominated the far wall, a richly imagined, opulently hued rendition of the view outside these very windows, give or take a handful of centuries, painted by no less an artist than Titian.

Murano glass vases glowed scarlet and blue on the dresser, picking up the light from the Venetian chandelier that hung from the ceiling high above. Bethany knew that one of this room's more famous occupants hundreds of years ago had been the daughter of a grand

and noble Venetian family, and this room had ever since been adapted to pay homage to her residency.

What legacy might Bethany have left behind, she wondered, had she stayed? Would she have left her mark at all or would she have been swallowed whole into this castle, this family, this history? Annoyed by her sentimentality, and that wrenching sense of loss that inevitably followed, she shook the thought away.

She pretended she was not aware of Leo still standing in the doorway that connected his suite to hers. She pretended she could not feel the weight of his gaze and the far heavier and more damaging crush of the memories she fought to keep from her mind tugging at her, pulling at her, making her feel as if she waded through molasses.

Yet, despite herself, she was attuned to his every movement, his every breath.

"Dinner will be served at eight o'clock," he said in his inexorable way when the silence in the room seemed to pound in her ears. "And, yes, we still maintain tradition and dress for dinner."

She turned back toward him, hoping the fact that she was wearing jeans annoyed him as much as it had three years ago, when he had had his social secretary admonish her for her relentlessly common fashion-sense. She had been seen wearing them in the village, where anyone might have recognized her—oh, the horror.

"As you are not a student but the *Principessa di Felici*, it would be preferable if you dressed in a manner more befitting your station," the dry, disapproving Nuncio had told her.

She reminded herself that she had only moments ago claimed to have grown up; such spiteful, petty thoughts rather undermined that claim.

She smiled with as much politeness as she could muster and waved a hand toward her bag where it stood near the door.

"As you can see, I brought very little," she said. "I doubt I have anything appropriate. I am more than happy to take a tray in my room."

"There is no need," Leo said smoothly, a smile playing near his sensual lips.

He moved then, his long strides bringing him far too close to her until he stopped at the large dressing-room that led away from the bed chamber itself. He opened the door and indicated the interior with a slight nod.

"Your wardrobe remains intact."

Bethany felt her mouth open and snapped it closed.

"You cannot mean…?" She blinked. "I have been gone for three years."

Leo's smile deepened. "Eight o'clock," he said softly.

She did not know why she should feel so… disarmed. She did not know why it felt as if he had kept her things out of some sense of emotional attachment to her—when she knew such a thing to be impossible. Leo did not have emotional attachments, to her or to anyone. It was far more likely that he had simply forgotten this room existed the moment she'd left and the contents of her closet along with it.

Still, she felt a fluttering in her stomach and a kind of ache in her chest.

Leo was too close now, within a single step, and she knew the exact moment that both of them realized that: the air seemed to disappear even as it heated. His eyes grew darker, more intent. His smile took on an edge that made a tight coil of need twist inside of her.

"No," she said, but it was little more than a whisper. Need. Longing. She did not know which was worse.

"What are you refusing?" he asked, taunting her. "I have offered you nothing."

Yet, was the unspoken next word. It seemed to shimmer between them. Bethany could imagine his hands cupping her face, his hard, impossible mouth on hers. She knew exactly how it would feel, exactly how deeply and fully she would feel it.

But she knew better than to let him touch her. She knew better than to trust herself this close to him. It was not him she feared, it was herself. Once she touched him again, how could she ever stop?

"I am here for one reason, Leo," she said, wanting to back away from him but worried that doing so would make her look weak, and encourage him to push his advantage. "I am not here to dress in fancy gowns for lavish dinners I do not want, much less to play bedroom games with you."

"Bedroom games?" His voice was like chocolate, dark and sweet. "I am intrigued. What sort of games do you have in mind?"

"A divorce," she said, feeling desperate. He still had yet to move! He simply looked at her in that knowing, shattering way, and it made her shiver. Her body wanted everything he had to offer and more. It always had. "All I want is a divorce. That is the only thing I have on my mind."

"So you have mentioned, I think," Leo said in that low, rich voice that seemed to connect directly to her nerve endings, sending sensations rippling throughout her limbs. "Repeatedly."

There was no magic, she told herself fiercely. He was not magical. It was simply because she was here, in this room, in this castle, in Italy. It was not his voice. It was not *him*. It was only the past, yet again.

If she turned her head too quickly she feared she would see her own ghost and his entwined together—on the thick rug beneath their feet, up against the door, on the window seat. They had always been insatiable. As their marriage had worn on and worsened, that had often been their only form of communication.

But those were ghosts, and this was now, and she knew exactly what that light in his eyes meant.

"I am sorry if I have begun to bore you," she managed to say. "A solution, of course, is to allow me to remain in this room until we go to court. You need never see me until then."

She sounded desperate to her own ears, yet Leo only smiled, a lazy, knowing smile that sent heat spiraling through her until her toes curled inside her shoes. It would be far too easy simply to move toward him. She knew he would catch her. He would sweep her into his arms and she would lose herself completely in that raging wildfire that was his to command.

A huge part of her wanted that, needed that, more than she wanted anything else—even her freedom. And that terrified her.

If she touched him, if she pressed her lips to his, she would forget. She would forget everything, as if it had all been a nightmare and he was the light of day. Wasn't that exactly what he'd done for her after her father had died? But she had no idea how she would ever fight her way out of it—not again. Not whole.

And she could not be this broken again. Not ever again.

"That would not suit me at all," he said, his attention focused on her mouth. "As I think you know."

"I don't want you to touch me!" she threw at him from the depths of her fear, her agony and her broken heart. Because she knew beyond a shadow of a doubt that she could not trust herself, not where he was concerned. She still wanted him too much. She bit her lip but then pulled herself together somehow, even as his arrogant brows climbed high.

"I beg your pardon?" He was all hauteur, untold centuries of nobility.

"You heard me." She looked around as if there was anything that might redirect her focus when he was standing so close. She sucked in a breath and returned her gaze to his. "The chemistry between us is damaging. It can only lead to confusion."

"I am not confused," he offered, smirking slightly.

"I do not want you," she lied, in a matter-of-fact voice. She did not smile; she met his gaze. "Not in that way. Not at all."

She expected his temper. His disbelief. She was unprepared for the full force of his devastating smile. He crossed his arms over his tautly muscled chest and gazed at her almost fondly. Somehow, that was far worse than any sardonic expression. It made her almost yearn.

"You are such a liar," he said softly, without heat. Flustered, she began to speak, but he cut her off. "You want me, Bethany. You always have and you always will, no matter what stories you choose to tell yourself."

"Your conceit is astonishing," she said even as her heart leapt in her chest and her legs felt shaky underneath her. Even as she felt the roll and sway, the seductive pull, of all that grief just beneath.

"Just as I want you," he said, shrugging as if it was of no matter to him—as, she reminded herself forcefully, it doubtless was not. "It is inconvenient, perhaps, but nothing more dangerous than that."

"Leo, I am telling you—" she began, feeling flushed and edgy.

"You need not concern yourself," he interrupted her, his words casual, almost offhand, though his gaze burned. "I have no intention of seducing you into my bed. In fact, I will not touch you at all as long as you are here."

She stared at him, letting those unexpected words sink in, telling herself that this was exactly what she wanted to hear, that this would make everything easy, that this was what she wanted. Though she could not entirely ignore the empty feeling that swamped her suddenly, nearly taking her off her feet.

"I am happy to hear that," she said. His eyes seemed to see straight through her and she was as terrified of what he might see as of what she might feel. What she already felt.

His smile took on that edge again and the tension between them seemed to crackle with new electricity, making it hard to breathe.

"I will leave it to you," he said in that compelling voice of his that slid like whiskey and chocolate over her, through her, inside of her.

"To me?" She could hardly do more than echo him.

"If you want me, Bethany, you must come to me." His deep-brown eyes were mesmerizing, so dark and rich, with that gold gleam within.

His voice lowered. "You must be the one to touch me, not the other way around."

"That will work perfectly," she said, her voice betraying her by cracking even as her breasts and her hidden core grew heavy and ached, yearned. "As I have absolutely no intention—"

"There are your intentions and then there is reality," he said smoothly. His gaze sharpened suddenly, catching her off-guard. "You cannot keep your hands off me. You never could. But you prefer to pretend that the passion between us is something I use to control you. Is that not what you said so memorably? That I would prefer it if I could keep you chained to my bed? It certainly makes you feel more the martyr to think so."

Bethany's mouth fell open then. There was a heat behind her eyes and a riot in her limbs as she tried to make sense of what he was saying—what he was doing or, more to the point, deliberately not doing.

"I am not a martyr," was all she could think to say, instantly wishing she could yank the words back into her mouth. She did not feel like a martyr, she felt adrift and unsteady, as she had always felt here.

"Indeed you are not," he said softly, deliberately, that gleam in his eyes growing hard, seeming to take over the room, her pounding heart. "What you are is a liar. It is entirely up to you to prove otherwise."

He thought she was a liar. He had said it before, and she had no doubt he meant it. It was almost amusing, she thought, unable to look away from him for a long, searing moment. It should have been amusing, really, and she wanted to laugh it off, but she found she had no voice. She could not seem to find it.

She could not reply in kind, or at all, and she did not know why that seemed to highlight everything they'd lost. What was being called a liar next to all of that?

"Eight o'clock," he said with a certain finality and evident satisfaction. "Do not make me come and fetch you."

Then he walked from the room and left her standing there, shocked, trembling and lost again, so very lost—as he had no doubt planned from the start.

There was so much she had forgotten, Bethany thought as she made her way through the castle's quiet halls toward dinner moments before eight o'clock, as requested.

She had not expected to find so many memories when she'd ventured into her former closet and searched for something simple to wear to dinner. It was not quite a homecoming, and yet every gown, every bag, every shoe had seemed to whisper a different half-forgotten story to her.

They had all come flooding back to her without warning, leaving her raw and aching for a past she knew she needed to keep firmly behind her if she was to escape it. But the memories had rushed at her anyway.

A night out at the opera in Milan, where the glorious voices had seemed to pale next to the fire in Leo's gaze that she'd believed could burn out everything else in the world. A weekend at a friend's villa outside of Rome, replete with sunshine and laughter—and with her growing fear that she was losing him a constant sharpness underneath.

A rare public eruption of his fiercely contained temper on a side street in Verona while walking to a business dinner, quick, brutal and devastating. A passionate moment on a quiet bridge in Venice; the explosive, impossible desire that still shimmered between them had been the only way left to reach each other across the walls of bitterness and silence they'd erected.

So many images and recollections, none of which she had entertained in ages, all of them buffeting her, storming her defenses, making her feel weak, small, vulnerable in ways she hadn't been in years.

She ran her hands along the swell of her hips as she walked, smoothing the silken, kelly-green material that flowed to her feet, trying to calm herself. The simple cowl-necked dress was the only item she'd been able to find that was both relatively restrained and unconnected to any of the explosive memories she had not known she'd been carrying around with her.

But it was not only the memories connected to her forgotten clothes that had unnerved her.

More than that, she'd realized during that confusing interaction with Leo that on some level she had forgotten who she was back then. The woman Leo had referred to so disparagingly—the one who had behaved so appallingly, who had, she was humiliated to recall, more than once destroyed more than one piece of china while in a temper—was not her.

That was not who she was, not anymore. It made her stomach hurt to think of it. To think of who he must see when he looked at her. To think that she remembered her isolation and the loss of all she had loved, but he remembered nothing but a termagant.

It had been that last night that had changed her, she realised, as she descended the great stone stair that dominated the front hall, rising from both sides to meet in the center and then veer off to the east and west wings. That last, shameful night. It was as if something had broken in her then, as if she'd been faced with the depths of her own temper, her own depraved passions. She'd lost that fiery, inconsolable part of herself, that wild, violent, mad part. For good? she thought.

Or perhaps it is Leo who stirs up all those dark and disgraceful urges, an insidious voice whispered. Perhaps he is the match. Perhaps without him you are simply tinder in a box, harmless and entirely free of fire.

"I am shocked," came his lazy drawl, as if she'd summoned him simply by thinking of him.

Bethany's head snapped up and she found Leo standing at the foot of the great stair, his brown eyes fathomless as he watched her approach.

"I had anticipated you would ignore what I told you and force me to come and deliver you to the table myself," he continued, and she knew there was a part of him that wished she had done just that. Because there was a part of her that wished it too.

"As I keep attempting to explain to you," she said, forcing a smile that seemed to scrape along all the places she was raw, "You do not know me any longer."

"I am sure that is true," he said, but there was an undercurrent in his rich voice that made her wonder what he did not say.

It was so unfair that he was who he was, she thought in a kind of despair as she continued to walk toward him, step by stone step.

The walls were covered with heavy tapestries and magnificent portraits of the Di Marco family from across the ages. Every step she took was an opportunity to note the well-documented provenance of the thrust of Leo's haughty cheekbones, the fullness of his lips, the flashing, dark richness of his gaze, all laid out for her in an inexorable march through the generations. His height, his rangy male beauty, his thick and lustrous hair: all of this was as much his legacy as the castle they both stood in.

And he was not only the product of this elegant, aristocratic line—he was its masterpiece. Tonight he wore a dark suit she had no doubt he had had made to his specifications in one of Milan's foremost ateliers, so that the charcoal-hued fabric clung to his every movement. He was a dream made flesh, every inch of him a prince and every part of him devastatingly attractive. It was hardwired into his very DNA.

How could she explain to this man what it was to feel isolated? He was never alone; he had servants, aides, dependants, villagers, employees. Failing that, he had some eight centuries of well-documented family history to keep him company. He was always surrounded by people in one way or another.

Bethany had only had her father since she'd been tiny, and then she'd had only Leo. But soon she had lost him too, and it had broken her in ways she knew that he—who had never had no one, who could not conceive of such a thing—would never, ever understand. She only knew that she could not allow it to happen a second time or she was afraid she would disappear altogether.

"Why do you frown?" he asked quietly, his gaze disconcertingly warm, incisive—dangerous.

"Am I?" Bethany tried to smooth her features into something more appropriate as she finally came to a stop on the step just above him—something more uninviting, more appropriate for a divorcing couple. "I was thinking of all these portraits," she said, which was not untrue, and waved a hand at the walls. "I was wondering when yours will grace the walls."

"On my fortieth birthday," he replied at once, his brows arching. He smirked slightly, and his tone turned sardonic. "Do you have an artist in mind? Perhaps your lover is a painter. What a delightful commission that would be."

Bethany pulled in a long breath, determined not to react to him as he obviously wished her to do. Determined not to feel slapped down, somehow—after all, she was the one who had introduced the concept of a lover into this mess. She was lucky Leo preferred to make sardonic remarks and was not altogether more angry, as she'd expected him to be. She was somewhat mystified he was not.

She forced another smile, hiding the sharp edges she did not wish to feel, pretending they did not exist.

"I only wondered how odd it must be to grow up under the gaze of so many men who look so much like you," she said. "You must never have spent even a moment imagining who you might be when you grew up. You already knew exactly what was in store for you."

She looked at the nearest painting, a well-known Giotto portrait of one of the earliest Di Marco princes, who looked like a shorter, rounder, eccentrically clad version of the man in front of her.

"I am my family's history," he said matter-of-factly, yet not without a certain resolute pride.

She could feel the current of it in him, around him. "I am unintelligible without it."

He spoke in an even sort of tone, as if he expected her to fight him about it. Had she done that before? she wondered suddenly. Had she argued simply for the sake of arguing? Or had she simply been too young then to understand how any history could shape and mold whomever it touched? She wondered if some day she would think about their complicated history without the attendant surge of anger and the darker current of grief.

"I can see that living here would make you think so," she agreed and turned her attention back to him in time to see a curious expression move through his eyes, as if he felt the same currents, then disappear.

"Our dinner awaits," he said softly. "If you are finished with my ancestors?"

She descended the last few stairs and fell into step with him when he began to walk. The castle seemed so immense all around them, so daunting. Shimmering chandeliers lit their way, spinning light down from the high ceilings, showcasing the grace and beauty of every room they walked through.

"Do we dine alone?" she asked in the same quiet tone he had used, though she was not certain why she felt a kind of pregnant hush surround them. She cleared her throat and tried to contain her wariness. "Where are your cousins?"

He glanced at her, then away. "They no longer call the castello their home."

"No?" So polite, Bethany thought wryly, when she had nothing at all courteous to say about Leo's spiteful, trouble-making cousins. She had been so delighted when she'd met them; as the only child of two deceased only-children, she'd been excited she would finally experience 'family' in a broader sense. "I was under the impression that they would never leave here."

Leo looked down at her, his gaze serious as they moved through a shining gold and royal blue gallery. They headed toward the smaller reception rooms located in the renovated back of the castle that, as of the eighteenth century, opened up to a terrace with a view out over the valley.

"They were not offered any choice in the matter," he said, a trace of stiffness in his voice. Almost as if he finally knew what she had tried to tell him back then. Almost as if…

Bethany searched his face for a moment, then looked away.

Both the cruel, beautiful Giovanna and the haughty, unpleasant Vincentio had hated—

loathed—Leo's spontaneous choice of bride. And neither had had the slightest qualm about expressing their concerns. The noble line polluted. Their family name forever contaminated by Leo's recklessness.

But Leo had not allowed a word to be spoken against them, not in the year and a half that they had made Bethany's life a misery. And now he had banished them from Felici?

She was afraid to speculate about what that might mean, afraid to let herself wonder, even as that treacherous spark of hope that still flickered deep inside of her threatened to bloom into a full flame. She doubted she would survive placing her hopes in Leo again. The very idea of it was sobering.

He did not lead her to one of the more formal rooms as Bethany had anticipated. She had not, of course, anticipated they might dine in the great dining hall itself, which was equipped to serve a multitude, but had imagined the more intimate family dining-room that was still elegant enough to cow her. But Leo did not stop walking until they reached the blue salon with its bright, frescoed ceilings and high, graceful windows.

Through the French doors that opened off the room, Bethany could see a small wrought-iron table had been set up on the patio to overlook the twinkling lights of the village and the valley beyond. The Italian night was soft all around her as she stepped outside, alive with the scent of cypress and rhododendrons, azaleas and wisteria. She could not help taking a deep, fragrant breath and remembering.

The table was laden with simple, undoubtedly local fare. Bethany knew the wine would be from the Di Marco vineyards, and it would be full-bodied and perfect. The olives would have been hand-picked from the groves she could see from her windows. The bread smelled fresh and warm, and had likely been baked that morning in the castello's grand kitchens.

A simple roasted chicken sat in the center of the table, fragrant with rosemary and garlic, flanked by side dishes of mushroom risotto and a polenta with vegetables and nuts. Candles flickered in the night air, casting a pool of warm, intimate light around the cozy, inviting scene.

Bethany swallowed and carefully took the seat that Leo offered her. She felt a deep pang of something like nostalgia roll through her, shaking her. It was worse in its way than the usual grief, but by the time Leo took his place opposite her she was sure she had hid it.

"This is by far the most romantic setting I

could have imagined," she said, a feeling of desperation coiling into a tense ball in her belly.

Why was he torturing her like this? What was the point of this meal, of their elegant attire, of this entire charade?

She met his gaze, though it took more out of her than she wanted to admit, even to herself. "It is more than a little inappropriate, don't you think? This is the first night of our divorce, Leo."

Leo did not respond at once, letting her words sit there between them. There was something almost brittle in the way she sat opposite him, as if she were on the verge of shattering like glass. He was not certain where the image had come from, nor did he care for it.

The Bethany he knew was vocal, mercurial. She did not break; she bent until she'd twisted herself—and him—into new and often contradictory shapes. He was not at all sure what to do with a Bethany he could not read, a Bethany whose temper he could not predict with fatalistic accuracy.

He was even less sure how it made him feel.

He reached over and poured the wine, a rich and aromatic red, into both of their glasses.

"Can we not enjoy each other's company, no

matter the circumstances?" he asked. "Have we really fallen so far?"

He let his gaze track the flush that tinted her skin slightly red, and made the deep, inviting green of her dress seem that much more beckoning. He wanted to reach across the table and test the curls that fell from the twist she'd secured to the crown of her head, but refrained. When he gave his word, he kept it.

No matter what it cost him.

"It is questions like that which make me question your motives," she said, a vulnerable cast to her fine mouth. She kept her gaze trained on him as he lounged back in his chair and merely eyed her in return, trying to figure her out, trying to see beyond the facade.

He was starting to wonder why she was so determined to divorce him—and why she refused even to discuss it. It was almost as if she feared he would talk her out of it, should she allow the conversation. Which, of course, he would.

Talk or no talk, there would be no divorce. He wondered why he did not simply announce this truth to her here and now and do away with the suspense. He knew he would have done so three years ago without a second thought.

Was it a weakness in him that he was content to let this play out—that he was intrigued despite himself by this new version of his wife? Her return, her uncertainty, her obvious response to him that she worked so hard to conceal…he found himself fascinated by it all. He did not want to crush her with a truth he suspected she would claim to find unbearable. He wanted to see what happened between them first.

He did not want to investigate why that was. He did not want to look too closely at what felt more and more like an indulgence with every passing second.

He began to realize exactly what he had done by vowing he would not touch her. Perhaps she was not the only one who had hidden in their explosive passion. Perhaps he too had used it as a shorthand—a bridge. It was an unsettling notion.

But this time, he thought with a certain grimness, he would make sure that there were no shortcuts taken. They would achieve the same destination, but this time they would both do it with their eyes wide open. It was the only way he could be sure that there would be no more years of estrangement, no more talk of divorce. And the more he let this play out, he told himself, the less likely that there could be arguments from Bethany about compulsion and manipulation, and all the rest of the accusations she levied at him.

"You are so focused on our divorce," he said after a moment. He selected a plump, ripe olive from the small bowl, swimming in oil and spices. He popped it in his mouth. "Don't you think we should first discuss our marriage?"

She let out a startled laugh. Her blue eyes looked shocked, which irritated him far more than it should have done. As if *he* was the unreasonable one, the hysterical one!

"You want to…talk?" she asked. Her tone of amazement set his teeth on edge. "You, Leo Di Marco, want to talk. Now. After all this time."

Something that looked like pain washed through her extraordinary eyes—but it could not be; how could it be? Then it was gone, hidden once more behind that brand-new armor of hers that she wore far too comfortably for his tastes.

"There was a time I might have killed to hear you say such a thing," she said after a moment, her voice husky. Her mouth twisted slightly, wryly. "But that is long past, Leo. It is too late for talking now, so far after the fact. Surely you see that?"

"Three years have passed since we were last together," Leo said, unperturbed, keeping his attention focused on her face. She looked away and he felt the loss, as if she had deliberately shut him out. "I imagine that ought to provide us the necessary distance."

"The distance to do what?" she asked— almost wistfully, he thought. She was still gazing out at the dark gardens, a faint frown between her brows. "Rake over the old coals? Poke around for old wounds? I do not understand the purpose of such an exercise. What will it accomplish? Our scars are our scars. Must we compare them?"

He searched her face, so much like a stranger's, when he had once thought he'd known it and its secrets far better than he knew his own.

He did not understand his own feelings. He wanted to go to her, to comfort her, and he could not understand the urge. The need for her body, for that addictive fire that raged between them—that he comprehended fully. But why should he want to chase the shadows from her eyes? Why should he yearn to make her smile? He wanted to focus on her duties, her obligations, the role he expected her to play. The rest of it, these softer urges, led directly to places within himself he had no desire to visit. He had walled them off long ago.

"You have returned after a long absence," he said, feeling as if he moved across shards of broken glass, buried mines. As if any wrong move might shatter them both.

He was aware of the tension rising between them and aware that it was not sexual in origin. He knew better than to let down his walls and feel, as he had once allowed himself to do so disastrously in the seductive tropics of Hawaii. Yet he could not seem to block her as he knew he should.

She shifted in her seat and her fingers crept up to her neck, as if she held her own pulse in her hand. Her eyes seemed huge and bruised, somehow, in the candlelight.

"I have not exactly returned, have I?" she said quietly, her gaze mysterious, compelling, more like the sea now than the summer sky. "Not really. Soon it will be as if I never came to this place at all."

"If that is what you want," he replied just as quietly, aware of the soft night all around them and the sense of change, of some kind of promise, in the air.

He wanted to see into her. He wanted to know her secrets, finally, and in so doing vanquish the ghost of her that haunted him even now while she sat within reach.

He wanted to reach out, but did not.

Could not.

He would not let himself, because it felt too

much like it had so long before in Hawaii, when he had fallen too hard and trusted too much, and he had vowed he would never give into that weakness again. Not even for her.

CHAPTER SIX

"I WANT a great many things," Bethany said, lulled by the strangest sensation of something almost like peace that hovered between them. It made her wonder. It made her reckless. It tempted her to forget. "But I am finally old enough to understand that not everything I want is good for me."

If she expected him to smile, or nod in agreement, she was disappointed. He only stared at her for a long moment, then shook his head slightly, dispelling the odd feeling.

"From that I am to gather that it is your marriage you find… What is it?" He affected a total lack of understanding, as if it was perhaps the English she knew very well he spoke fluently that eluded him. She felt it like a slap. "Bad for your health?"

It was Leo at his most patronizing and it reminded her forcibly of the reason why she was here—not to understand what had happened between them, but to put it behind her once and for all.

She sighed, annoyed at herself for her momentary lapse, and busied herself with filling her plate. At least she knew that everything that was offered to her in this place would be excellent. Nothing else would be tolerated. She took a few slices of the chicken, and could not resist a large helping of the creamy risotto.

"No answer?" he asked quietly. He let out a sound somewhere between a laugh and a sigh. "Why am I not surprised?"

Bethany straightened her shoulders and took a calming breath as she picked up her fork. "As it happens, I have given the matter some thought," she said evenly. As if she was unaware he was coiled in his chair, waiting to strike. "I believe that when a marriage diminishes and degrades the people in it—" she began.

He actually laughed then, cutting her off.

"Such strong words," he taunted her. "You feel degraded, Bethany? I degrade you?" He shook his head, his eyes glittering, as if she had accused him of a terrible crime—as if was not the simple truth.

"You are the one who wanted a discussion, Leo," she threw back at him, exasperated, and unable to completely repress her reaction to him even under these circumstances. What was the matter with her? "You should have made it clear you meant that discussion to be entirely on your terms, as ever! I can do without your scorn."

"What you would like to do without is the truth," he said, all pretense of laughter gone from his hard face. The candles cast his features into harsh angles, forbidding shadows. "Because the truth is that you do not come out the victim in this scenario. The fact that you have cast yourself in that role is one more example of the infantile behavior you claim to have left behind you."

"You are proving my point," she said, unable to keep the faint tremor from her voice. Even so, she kept her spine ramrod straight, determined to look strong no matter how she might feel when he ripped into her.

He studied her for a moment and Bethany felt her face heat. Anger, she told herself. It was nothing more than anger, and never mind the twisting ache inside. Never mind the contradictory, baffling urge to reach out to him, to bridge the gap between them, no matter what it cost her.

"Perhaps it is simply that you are too fragile to face up to who you really are," he said softly. Deliberately.

She let out a small laugh and then put down her fork, no longer able even to pretend to enjoy the food, no matter how perfectly prepared.

"Who are you to tell me who I really am?" she asked with a kick of temper, clenching her hands into fists below the table, where he could not see. She had longed for him to know her, to see her, for years—but he never had. She shook away the old wants, the old needs, even as they seemed to sear through her, leaving deep marks behind. "When you are the person who knows me least of all?"

"I know you," he said, with that terrifying ring of finality, of certainty, that she could sense meant things to him that she was better off not knowing. "I know you in ways no one else could."

"If that was ever true, it has not been true for a long time," she replied, choosing her words carefully. Trying to ignore the part of her that still desperately wanted him to know her the way he claimed he did, the part of her that wished so deeply that somehow, some way, he could.

She shook her head, trying to ward off her own turmoil and his accusatory glare.

"Let me guess," he said icily. He did not move, and yet she could feel the way his gaze, his attention and temper focused on her, narrowing in on them both, trapping them in the grip of this roiling tension between them. "No doubt you have spent the past three years coming up with the perfect, bloodless fantasy to use as a comparison to our relationship. No doubt your supernaturally forgiving lover aids you in this. Anything to avoid looking at yourself with any form of honest appraisal, is that it?"

Her temper flared. And for once she could think of no particular reason to keep it locked up. She told herself she had nothing to lose—it was all already lost. This was simply a pointless dance around the bonfire of what they had been. An opportunity to watch it all burn away into ash.

So why should she bite her tongue?

"I do not think marriage should be a monarchy, with you installed as king by divine right while I am expected to play the role of grateful, subservient subject," she told him, the words three years in the making. For a brief moment she felt just as she sounded. Calm. Deadly. "It cannot even be called a marriage. It is an exercise in steamrolling, and I am tired of feeling flattened by you."

They stared at each other for a long moment. His expression was frozen, arrested. She was aware of the slight breeze against her bare skin, the dance of the candles in their crystal holders. She was not holding her breath, not quite. She felt as if she watched the scene from on high.

She had never dared say such things to Leo before. How could she? Their relationship had been entirely based on his acknowledged superiority. What room had there been for her to call his actions or his assumptions into question?

And she knew that her own appalling behavior had only made everything worse. Who would have listened to an out-of-control maniac who smashed things? Who would take the emotional mess seriously? Certainly not Leo.

And not even herself, Bethany acknowledged with no little pain. That had come later.

"You say the most extraordinary things," he said coldly.

Because Leo did not explode. Leo did not rage, yell or allow things to become messy. Leo did not, could not, feel.

"I understand that this is all a foreign concept to someone who has issued orders to his minions from his cradle," she said, her voice stiff from her own revelations, and only partially a response to his chilly glare, no matter how it pierced her. "Who has priceless paintings on his walls of his own family members. Who lives in a castle."

"You quite mistake me," he bit out. "I am

astonished that you would have any thoughts at all on what might make for a good marriage. Real relationships are not conducted according to your every melodramatic whim and tantrum, Bethany."

"That's taking the concept of the pot calling the kettle black to the level of farce," she replied, blinking away the avalanche of emotion that threatened to drag her under. There was no room for that here, now. And she could not be certain what lurked just on the other side.

His mouth flattened with displeasure, but she did not back down. Because, no matter what he believed, it was true.

He had left her to die of loneliness, and she nearly had.

"I am not the one who issued ultimatums and then, when they were not met, threw temper tantrums," he said then. His mouth twisted; his dark eyes were condemning. "I am not the one who stubbornly refused contact for years in an extended fit of pique."

"Stop it!" she hissed, but he gave no sign of hearing her. She had the sense that he had been waiting to say these things as long as she had. She could see the way he held himself, all that power and ferocity tightly leashed and controlled, even now.

"I am also not the one who issued a demand

for a divorce instead of the polite greeting one might give a stranger on the street." His eyes seemed to glow with his cold, consuming fury. He was, she realized, more angry than she had imagined. More angry than she had ever seen him. Was it sick that she wanted that to mean something? "And having done all of those things, seemingly without shame, I am not the one to sit here now and lecture on about successful marriages."

She wanted to scream at him, to protest what he'd said, but how could she? She had done all of those things. Could he not see how he had driven her to it? How she had never had any other choice? How she had felt forced to flee— or she might have withered away to nothing but an empty shell?

"I have always been right here, Bethany," he said, the anger she had never imagined she would see in him lighting him with a cold glow, making her yearn to warm him somehow, despite herself. "Right here, awaiting your return, should you ever condescend to recall your commitments."

"I don't know why you would expect—" she began, but cut herself off, her mind reeling. How could she ever imagine he might see these things from her perspective?

He saw only her abandonment of him. He

never saw his own abandonment of her, because he had not physically left her. He had only disappeared in every other possible way. Yet he still considered himself firmly on the moral high ground.

"You to keep your promises?" he finished for her, his voice heavy with irony. When his gaze met hers it was too intense and angry, kicking into her and making her stomach clench and her breath catch. "Because you gave your word."

She wanted to fight him, deny his condemnation—but she was much too afraid that was not what she really wanted. That beneath it, she only wanted those dark eyes to shine at her again, as they had once. And she could not let herself down that way. Not this time. Not again.

"You gave your word too," she said in a determined undertone. "But that did not prevent you from conveniently—"

"Did I beat you?" he asked, his voice raw, yet still so fiercely controlled. Only his eyes showed any hint of the wildness within, so dark and stormy, bittersweet and on fire. "Did I take other women to my bed? Did I abuse you? Demean you? Did I fail to attend to your every need?"

He waved a hand at the castello.

"Is my home not big enough? Is it too rural? Would you prefer the house in Milan? Exactly what is the root of all this bitterness and hostility?" he demanded. "What did I do that was so terrible you punished me in the only way you could—by running away?"

She could not breathe for a long moment, could not manage it past the swell of agony that swept through her. When she could, she had to fight off tears. Was that truly how he saw her—no more than a spiteful little brat? She knew with a sudden, unbearable certainty that it was. He believed she'd left him on a whim—rather than in pieces.

"I can't imagine why you ever wanted me in the first place," she managed to say, her voice trembling, shaken to the bone.

"Oh, I want you." His voice was far too raw then, with too many undercurrents, and spoke to all the sins she dared not name—all of which he had taught her. The look in his eyes set her afire. His expression was almost brooding. Something deeper, more painful, than simply *wry*. "It seems there is nothing at all you can do to keep me from wanting you, and you have certainly put that to the test."

He did not move, he only watched her, and yet he seemed, suddenly, to be everywhere. It was as if she had forgotten the danger of being this close to him—of talking to him, of allowing him to weave his way into her psyche again—until this very second—and now she could notice nothing else.

Her heart beat in a jagged rhythm. Her mouth was far too dry. She felt as if her entire body was short-circuiting, shutting down. Readying itself for his touch.

It did not matter how much it hurt. She still wanted him. She always wanted him.

Blindly, she shoved away from the table and lurched to her feet. She knew only that she had to escape. She had to put distance between them, because he might have made a promise not to touch her of his own volition, but she knew all too well that she was the one who could not be trusted in that area.

She moved toward the French doors and she knew even as she reached for the handle that he was behind her. She did not have to turn and confirm it, not when she could *feel* him.

She stopped with her hand on the ornate handle and felt the heat of him at her back, so close she could smell the faintest hint of his cologne—so near that if she shifted her weight backward she would be nestled beneath his chin, her back against the hot, hard wall of his chest.

"You promised!" she whispered, desperate to run away and yet frozen in place. She wanted him, but she also wanted the comfort of his heat, his closeness, his scent.

He had been her man, her family, her love. She still did not know how to let go of any of that, only that she must.

Even so, her eyes drifted closed. "You said you would not…"

"Am I touching you?" he asked in that low, stirring tone that seemed to roll through her, quietly devastating her, reducing her to little more than mindlessness and need.

She turned then, before her knees collapsed beneath her, and found her back against the door with nothing before her but Leo. As if he was all the world.

He leaned closer, resting his hands against the paned glass on either side of her head, a move that brought his mouth nearly flush with hers.

And though she could feel him in every part of her—in her swollen breasts, her taut belly, her molten femininity—he did not touch her. He kept his promise. He only gazed down at her, his eyes hard with a passion she recognized all too well.

"I cannot stop wanting you," he said then, his mouth a breath away, his sensual lips close enough to kiss. "And I have tried. Nights I lay awake, cursing your name, and yet here I am—as ready for you as if there was no history between us, no years apart, no demands for a divorce."

"Leo…" But she could not seem to form any words save his name, even then, when she knew she should end this moment, whatever it was.

She should not let him speak these things out loud, making both of them remember. Making her yearn. Ache. *Want.*

But all she could do was stare up at him and hope her heart did not beat so hard, so frantically, that it might break through her own ribs as she half-feared it might.

"You are under my skin," he whispered as if it was torn from him. "You are like a poison. You cannot seem to kill me, but I cannot seem to be rid of you."

He had said too much, Leo thought, and yet he did not step back.

He could not seem to make his own body obey him, not when she was so close. He could feel her breath against his skin, close enough that he could smell the unique scent of her. Like lavender and vanilla—her own delectable perfume.

He could count the freckles that splayed across her nose, and knew what the larger one on her clavicle tasted like. He felt it when their breath began to move in sync, as it always had—as if their bodies insisted on synchronizing even as they dedicated themselves to remaining at war.

This close to her, he could not even remember why.

"You…" She could not manage to speak. He watched, fascinated, as she wet her soft lips and swallowed. "You must let me go."

"How many times must I let you go?" he heard himself whisper. Worse, he heard the emotion that was underneath it. The jagged pain. What was more horrifying was that he did not immediately move away from her. Not even then.

"You say you want me," she said in a low, urgent voice, her impossible blue eyes wide with a sheen that told him he was not the only one rubbed raw by this encounter, no matter that they were not actually touching.

"I do," he agreed. "Just as you want me, Bethany. I can feel it. I can see it."

"You say that," she continued as if it hurt her to push the words out. Her eyes searched his, something desperate there reaching out to him. "But you only want me if you can keep me in a convenient box of your choosing. If I behave, if I conform, if I act according to your rules, then I am treated like a queen. But it's still a box."

"You are confusing a box with a bed," he said. Her mouth was so close and her skin would be so soft and he could not believe he had made such a foolhardy promise, much less that he intended to keep it—even now when he was so hard it bordered on the painful.

"With you they are often the same thing," she said.

No matter how much he yearned simply to sink into her, he could not miss the reproving tone she used. He tilted his head back slightly and gazed at her, taking in that high red flush across her neck, the determined set of her jaw, the cool gleam in her eyes.

"I am only telling you the truth," she said after a long moment. She took a breath that lifted her breasts alluringly, but he refused to be sidetracked. "Nothing I did happened in a vacuum, Leo. You were as responsible for what happened in our marriage as I was. But I suppose it's easier to look only at me, isn't it?"

"I looked for you for three long years," he gritted out. He was so close to her it bordered on madness, yet he still did not touch her. "But you were never where you were supposed to be. Tell me what I was meant to do. Beg? Plead? Weep?"

"Why not?" she whispered fiercely. "Why not all of the above, if that is how you feel?"

"I am not you," he whispered back in the same hard tone, shoving through the things he refused to admit, even to himself. "I cannot flash my every emotion for all to see."

"You cannot or you will not?" She moved then, only slightly, but it brought her shoulder into glancing contact with his arm. They both froze, focused on that single, accidental touch. He watched her swallow, the long, graceful column of her throat begging for his mouth, his tongue, his teeth.

"Tell me to touch you," he ordered her huskily, their history forgotten in that moment like so much smoke. "Tell me to hold your face in my hands. Tell me to kiss you."

Her lips parted on a soundless breath, but he felt it fan across his jaw. Her eyes widened, darkened. He could feel that shimmering electricity arc between them, hot and wild.

"Tell me…" he whispered, moving his mouth to hover near her ear, so very close, just out of reach. "Tell me to take you in my arms and make you mine. Again and again. Until you cannot remember your name. Or my name. Or why you left."

* * *

She was almost his, until that last whispered sentence.

A chill snaked through her, and it gave her the strength to force open her eyes and remember. Why she was there. Why she could not simply surrender to him as every cell, every breath, every part of her longed to do. Why she could not let him cast this spell around her.

Not again.

"I think it is time for me to get some sleep," she said, keeping her head turned and choosing her words so carefully, so desperately. "I think the traveling is catching up with me."

He murmured something in Italian, something lyrical that she did not have to understand to know was all sex and command. She could feel it move between her legs, coil low in her belly and spiral along her skin until she shivered in reaction. But she did not look at him. She knew, somehow, that gazing into his eyes just then would be the end of her. She knew it.

"If that is what you wish," he said eventually, and he pushed away. The night air seemed to rush at her, cooler than it had been moments before; shocking.

He stood only a foot or two away, his beautiful face shadowed, though his eyes burned with a fire she dared not touch. Or even acknowledge.

"I will see you in the morning," she said with absurd, unnecessary courtesy.

His brows arched with a dark amusement, and she did not wait to see what he might say. Instead, she fled.

Again, she fled from him. She had spent her whole life running away from this man, it seemed. Was he right to accuse her as he had? Was he right to lay the blame at her feet?

She moved through the quiet halls as if pursued, though she knew he did not follow her. Not then. She closed the heavy door of her bedchamber tight behind her and did not so much as glance at the other door.

She did not let herself think about where it led or how easy it would be to simply walk through the doorway and succumb to what her body wanted—and what would be, she knew, so very easy. So deliriously easy. Far easier than these conversations that ripped apart scars she had thought long-healed.

She pulled off her gown, changed into the comfortable pajamas she had brought with her from Toronto, scrubbed her face until there was no hint of color left in her skin and crawled into the wide, empty bed.

It was as soft and inviting as she remembered. No place for terrifying, unwieldy emotions. No room for a very old grief.

But she did not get to sleep for a long, long time.

CHAPTER SEVEN

HE WAS waiting for her in the breakfast room the next morning.

She walked in, her head still a confused muddle from the night before, and there he was. The sunlight poured in through the high, arched windows and surrounded him with a golden halo, despite the fact he looked forbidding and unapproachable at the head of the table. His gaze rose to meet hers over the top of the paper he held before him, cool and remote, in direct contrast to the pool of light around him.

She knew perfectly well he was challenging her, and it hit her hard and true, like an electrical charge, sizzling directly into the coiled tension low in her belly and between her legs.

Somehow, Bethany managed to keep herself from stumbling in the high, wedged sandals she had foolishly opted to wear beneath a casual knit sundress. She could feel his gaze in every cell, along every nerve. She had to fight to breathe normally.

Pressing her lips together, she let the ever-present servant seat her with a solicitousness that struck her as an absurdly formal manner to take with the soon-to-be ex-wife. The room was bathed in light and seemed to shimmer with promise, from the painted medieval ceiling with its long, dark beams to the bright friezes that decorated the walls above the wainscoting.

She could sense more than feel Leo's long legs stretched out beneath the polished wooden table, too close to her own, and wished that it was bigger or that she was further away from him instead of having to share a corner with him. As it was, she sat at a diagonal to Leo. But her body was not about to let her pretend she was not attuned to every single detail of his distressingly perfect appearance, the power he exuded as easily as he drew breath and the in-credible, undeniable force of the pull he seemed to exert upon her.

Even now, when she had vowed to start anew this morning. When she had vowed not be so affected by him.

"Good morning," he said, and she was all too aware of the amusement that lurked in his gaze, his voice, the slight twist of his sensual lips.

Settled in her seat, the thick white linen

napkin draped over her lap, Bethany faced him fully, to offer the expected polite greeting that would prove her to be as unaffected as he was. To present him with the cool and calm façade that she knew she needed to use if she was to survive any of this intact.

But she froze when her eyes met his. The dark, passionate, starkly sexual dreams that had kept her half-awake and tormented with longing the whole of the endless night rose again in her head, taunting her. Shocking her. She could see all of that and more in his black-coffee gaze.

He did not merely look at her—he devoured her, his eyes hot and hard.

Hungry.

Her lips parted slightly as her breath deserted her. She felt her eyes glaze over, and that same tell-tale flush begin to heat its way along her breasts and neck.

It was as if he'd touched her, as if he was touching her *right now*—as if he'd reached over, yanked her into his lap and finally fixed that wicked mouth of his to hers. When all he had really done was greet her and then watch her, hard male satisfaction gleaming in his eyes and stamped across his beautiful, impossible face.

She did not need to be a mind reader to

realize that he knew exactly what her flush meant—that he suspected she had tossed and turned, her body aching for him, all night long. Leo knew exactly what he did to her—what she felt—simply because of his proximity.

He knew.

"All you need to do is touch me," he said now, his intoxicating voice slightly hoarse, as if his own *want* shook him as it shook her. "It would take so very little, Bethany. You need only reach your hand to mine. You need only—"

"Leo, please," she said, trying desperately to sound stern instead of weak, all too aware that she fell far short. "The only thing I want right now is coffee."

"Of course," he said, not even attempting to hide his sardonic amusement. "My apologies." He did not even need to call her a liar. It hung between them like a shout.

Bethany scowled at her plate as the efficient staff poured her thick, aromatic coffee and placed the toast and jam she had always favored before her. She did not want to think about the fact that her preferences still registered here. She would not consider the ramifications of that.

Instead, she somehow managed to keep her hands from shaking as she lifted her delicate china coffee cup to her lips and drank the rich brew. Only after she'd taken a few bracing, head-clearing sips could she bear to look at him again.

He had placed his newspaper to the side of his plate. He lounged back against his chair, his expression brooding, one hand supporting his jaw. He looked every inch the prince, the magnate, the duly crowned emperor of his vast and ever-expanding personal empire.

He wore another perfectly tailored suit, the charcoal fabric molded to his shoulders, pressed lovingly to his fine chest. He was freshly shaved, newly showered—his dark hair glossy, begging for her fingers to run through it. He was like a dream made flesh. Her dream, specifically. The explicit, delicious dream that had tortured her all night long.

But she could not reach across the divide between them, no matter how much she longed to do it. She could not allow herself to fall again, not when she knew exactly how hard that landing was. And how impossible it seemed to her that she would ever truly climb back to her feet and walk away from him.

"I must go to Sydney," he said into the simmering silence. She had the sense he picked his words carefully, for all his voice remained cool and unemotional. "There are fires to put out, I am afraid, and only I can do it."

"You are going to Australia?" she asked, jolted from her own depressing cycle of thoughts. "Today?"

"I am interested in some hotels there," he said. Again, with care. "We are at a delicate stage in the negotiations." He shrugged, though his gaze did not leave her face or soften at all. "I did not expect that I would have to attend to this personally."

Her mind raced. What exactly was he saying? But then, she knew. Hadn't she been here before? Repeatedly? There was always something, somewhere, that required his attention. A day here. A week there. Always at the last minute. Always non-negotiable.

"How long will you be gone?" she asked with as little expression as she could manage. She picked up a piece of perfectly toasted bread then dropped it again, unable to conceive of putting anything in her mouth when her throat felt too dry and her stomach clenched.

"It should not take long," he said, his own tone measured. He watched her, his expression cool.

"Which, if memory serves, can mean anything from an evening to two weeks," she said crisply. "A month? Six weeks? Who can say, when duty calls?"

He only lifted a brow and gazed at her, his

expression inscrutable. After a moment he lifted his hand and with a careless wave dismissed the hovering servants. The way he had always done—as a precaution, he had said once, so condescendingly,should she fly off the handle.

She gritted her teeth and shoved aside the humiliating memories. The tension that always swirled between them seemed to tighten, to pull at her, hard and hot.

"I sense this is a problem for you," he said with exaggerated patience.

He had said such things before, she recalled. *A problem for you.* The implication being, as ever, that only a hysteric like Bethany would ever dream of finding his business affairs personally objectionable. It made her want to scream.

But she would not give him the satisfaction of reducing her to that. She would tear out her own throat first.

"Why am I here?" she asked quietly. A sudden thought occurred to her and she could not hold it back. "Did you plan this?"

"It is business, Bethany," he said, his voice dismissive. "I know you choose to concoct plots and conspiracies wherever you look, but it is only business."

Any pretense of an appetite deserted her

and she stood, pushing her chair back with a loud screech as she rose to her feet. The high shoes she'd worn to make his height seem less impressive compared to her own now seemed precarious, but she refused to show it.

"I might as well go home to Toronto and continue living this mockery of a life," she began, as angry that she had not foreseen something like this as that he was behaving in the same manner he always had: putting his title above his wife.

"I cannot control the entire world, Bethany," he said in that tone she loathed, the one that made her feel like an out-of-control, embarrassing infant—the tone that had so often goaded her into becoming exactly that. "I would prefer not to have to leave you now that you have finally returned to Italy, but I must. What would you have me do? Lose billions because you are in a snit?"

She fought off the haze of fury that descended on her then, and did not care if he could see that her hands were clenched into fists at her sides. She wanted to do more than simply ball up her hands in futility. She wanted to scream. She wanted to reach him, somehow. She wanted to make him feel this small, this unimportant, this useless.

But that would be descending to levels she

never planned to visit again. She did not care that he stared at her while she fought her own demons. When she had battled herself into some semblance of control, she dared to look at him again.

"I understand that you need to speak to me this way," she said after a long moment. She was proud that her voice neither wavered nor cracked. "It even makes sense. Heaven forfend you treat me like an equal. Like a partner. That might make your own behavior subject to scrutiny, and the *Principe di Felici* cannot have that. Far better to manipulate the situation—to manipulate me into acting out the only way I could."

"You cannot be serious." He even let out a scoffing sort of laugh. "Is there nothing you are not prepared to throw at me? No accusation too big or too small?"

"You got to remain the long-suffering adult, while I got to be the screaming child," she continued as if he had not spoken. "It was a great disservice to both of us." She spread her palms wide as if she could encompass everything they'd destroyed, all they'd lost. "But I am not the same person, Leo. I am not going to break down into a tantrum so that you can feel better about yourself."

"All I have ever wanted is for you to act as

you should," he threw at her, no longer quite so languid. His jaw was set, his dark eyes glittering as he rose to his feet. They faced each other across the table, too close and yet, as ever, so very far apart. "But it seems to me I was nothing more than a replacement parent for you."

A surprising wave of grief for her lost father washed through her, combined with a different kind of grief for the things she had not realized she'd wanted when she had married this man.

The things she had not realized she had inadvertently asked for, that she had not liked at all when he'd provided them. Like this impossible, disastrous, circular dynamic that seemed to engulf them, that she could not seem to fight off or freeze out or flee from.

"But what about your behavior?" she managed to get out, fighting for control, her hold on her emotions tenuous as things she thought she'd never dare say flowed from her mouth. "Never a husband. Never a lover. Always the parent. What could I be, except a child?" She shook her head in astonishment—and censure. "And then you wanted to actually have one, too?"

"I must have an heir," he snapped, his expression frozen. "I never made any secret of that. You are well aware it is my primary duty as the *Principe di Felici.*"

"Let us not forget that," she threw back at him, her voice uneven to match the heaviness and wildness in her chest. "Let us not forget for even one moment that you are your duty first, your legacy second and only thereafter a man!"

"Is this what you learned in your years away, Bethany?" he asked after a brief, tense pause, his tone dangerous. Hard like a bullet. "This apportioning of blame?"

"I don't know who to blame," she admitted, the sea of emotion she'd fought to keep at bay choking her suddenly. "But it hardly matters anymore. We both paid for it, didn't we?"

When he did not speak, when he only gazed at her with fire and bitterness in equal measure, his mouth a grim line, she sighed.

Did his silence not say all there was to say? Wasn't this the tragic truth of their short marriage? He would not speak to her about the things that mattered, and he would not listen to her. She could only scream, and she could never reach him.

It hurt to look at it, so stark and unadorned in the bright morning sunshine. It hurt in ways she thought might take her lifetimes to overcome. But she would overcome this somehow. She would do more than simply survive him. She would.

"Go to Sydney, Leo," she said quietly, because there was nothing left to say. There never had been. "I do not care how long it takes. I will be here when you deign to return, ready and waiting to finally put all of this behind us."

Leo was in a towering rage, a fact he did nothing to conceal from his aides when they met his jet in Sydney and whisked him away to the sumptuous suite that awaited him at the hotel he no longer cared at all if he owned. He had stewed over Bethany's words the whole way from Milan, and had reached nothing even approaching a satisfying conclusion.

He started to worry that he never would—which was entirely unacceptable.

The picture she'd painted of their marriage had enraged him. It had infuriated him that night over dinner, and it had further incensed him this morning. Who was she to accuse him of such things, when her own sins were so great and egregious? When he was the one who had remained and she the one who had abandoned their marriage?

But his rage had eased the further he'd flown from the castello. His reluctance to be parted from her grew, no matter how angry she made him, and he found himself unable to maintain that level of fury.

Partly, it had been the brash courage written all over her face, as if she had had to fight herself to confront him in the way she had. He could not seem to force the image from his mind. Her remarkable eyes, blazing with bravado and no little trepidation. Her spine so straight, her chin high, her mouth set in a fierce line. Did it require so much strength to speak her mind to him, however off-base? Was he such a monster in her mind, after all they had shared?

What did that say about the kind of man he was? But he was afraid he already knew, and he did not care for the twist of self-recrimination that the knowledge brought him.

He could remember all too well his father's thundering voice booming through the halls of the Di Marco estates, the shouting and the sneering, his mother's bowed head and set, miserable expression. He remembered the way his mother had flinched away from the strong, cruel fingers on her upper arm. He remembered the curl of his father's lip when he had referred to her, when she'd not been in the room—and, worse, when she had been.

Leo did not like the juxtaposition at all.

But it was impossible, he told himself grimly. He was not Domenico Di Marco, the bully. He had never laid a finger on his wife. He had never done anything that should make any woman cower from him in fear, much less this particular woman. He had spent his life ensuring that he was absolutely nothing like his father.

Except… He remembered the look in Bethany's eyes three years ago. That misery. That fear. He had found it infuriating then—unacceptable that she could be so desperately miserable when he had given her so much and asked for so little in return. It had never crossed his mind that she might have had the slightest reason to feel that way.

She'd had no reason! he told himself angrily. Just as she has no basis for her accusations now!

Later, he sat in a boardroom packed with financial advisors and consultants who were paid to impress him. He pretended to watch yet one more presentation with the discerning eye for which he was so renowned. But he could not seem to concentrate on dry facts and figures, projections and market analysis. He could not seem to think of anything but Bethany.

I do not think marriage should be a monarchy, he heard her say over and over again on an endless loop in his brain. I am tired of feeling flattened by you.

His instinct was to dismiss what she said out of hand. She would say anything to try to hurt him. She had proven that to be true over and over again. She was interested in scoring points, that was all.

But he could not quite believe it.

It would have been one thing if she'd lapsed into her customary hysteria. It was so easy to ignore what she said when it was screamed or accompanied by a flying missile in the form of priceless china or ancient vases. But the Bethany who had faced him this morning had not flown off the handle, though she had been visibly upset by one more round in their endless, excruciating war.

She had fought for calm instead of succumbing to her temper and emotions, yet even so he had seen exactly how much that fight had cost her. He had seen the defeat and the pain written across her face as if, once more, he had disappointed her.

He wished that did not eat at him, but it did.

You only want me if you can keep me in a convenient box of your choosing, she had said. It resonated within him in a way he hated. She had accused him of wanting to be the father figure, the parent, the adult in their relationship. He had never wanted that, had he? That had been a reaction to her, hadn't it? Never a husband, she had said. Always the parent. What could I be, except a child?

A feeling he did not like at all snaked through him then as he accepted the fact that three years ago, he would not even have tried to figure out where she was coming from. He had not bothered.

He had simply let her go when it had occurred to him that perhaps the polish and experience of a few years' growth might work wonders for the brand new, far-too-young wife he had inexplicably taken, upsetting a lifetime's worth of expectations. He had been weary of all the fighting, all the wild uncertainty and drama. He had wanted her to turn into the wife he had been expected to marry all along, the wife he'd always been told he, as the *Principe di Felici*, needed to marry to fulfill his obligations. He had wanted her to be dutiful and unobjectionable.

What was that, if not a box? The very same box, in fact, in which he had lived his whole life?

The day's business was concluded in due course, and Leo sat through a tedious dinner with his soon-to-be new partners, forcing himself to play along with the expected joviality when he could not have felt less disposed to do so. Finally, after an endless round of drinks and toasts—that he found slightly premature, given the contracts that had yet to be signed and his lawyers' ability to ferret out objections to every clause they viewed—he was able to retire to his rooms and drop the act.

He had long ago stopped questioning how Bethany could haunt him so thoroughly in places she had never been. And yet, as he sat out on the balcony and soaked in the mild Sydney autumn night, it was as if she sat beside him, astride him. It was as if he could smell the rich, sweet scent of her skin, as if he could hear the cadence of her voice echo all around him, as if from the city itself.

Was every man doomed to become his father? He rejected the idea, but it was harder to push away than it should have been. Because, if he cast aside his own anger and frustration long enough, the view into their marriage from Bethany's perspective was not at all pretty. He had failed her.

He faced the truth of that and sighed slightly.

He had not protected her from his spiteful cousins, when he should have known the trouble they would cause with their insinuations and their ingrained snobbery. He had not properly prepared her for how different his daily life was from their Hawaiian idyll. And he had been the older, experienced one. He still was. It had surely been his responsibility to make sure she felt secure, safe, at home in a place that he knew had been wildly foreign to her. And he had not done it.

He had not done it.

He had been so quick to accuse her of all manner of ills, but he had never thought to examine his own behavior. Who was the child—the woman who had been so sheltered and naïve? Or the man who had such a high opinion of himself it had never occurred to him to see what responsibility lay at his feet for the mess of his own marriage?

Leo sat in the dark for a long time, staring out at the lights of the city, lost in his own thoughts. In the past. Deep in a pair of bright blue eyes he was determined he would see smiling once again, if it killed him.

CHAPTER EIGHT

"I DO NOT wish to put you in a box," Leo announced, striding into the small drawing room off the principessa's suite.

Bethany was so startled she dropped the book she was reading, letting the heavy first edition thud to the floor beside the gracefully bowed legs of the scarlet and white settee.

"Quite the contrary."

She had not seen him in days. Four days, to be precise.

She sat up, swinging her legs to the floor and straightening her shoulders as her eyes drank him in, as they always did and always had, no matter how angry and hurt she had been when he reappeared. She could not seem to help herself. Her heart leapt, no matter how sternly she lectured herself against such foolishness.

Since she could not control it, she tried instead to ignore it, and focused on him instead.

He looked…different, somehow. Bethany's

senses, more attuned to him than she was at all comfortable with, whispered an alert.

Leo's dark eyes glittered in a way that made the edgy need in her belly punch to life and roll lower, setting her alight. His mouth was set into a firm, determined line. He was dressed impeccably in a black jacket over a soft cashmere sweater, his legs packed into dark trousers. Even relatively casually dressed, he was fully the prince. Only he could look so regal so effortlessly.

"I am delighted to hear it," she said, eyeing him warily.

She felt vulnerable, somehow, as if she'd arranged herself on the settee simply to tempt him, with her curls in wild abandon and a soft wool throw over her bare feet. When, of course, she could not have known he would appear today. If she had, she would not have worn the casual denim jeans she knew annoyed him, much less the skimpy, tissue-thin T-shirt that she was afraid showed far more than it should.

She would have chosen far better armor to ward him off, to keep him at arm's length where he belonged.

As if he could read her as easily as she'd read the novel at her feet, Leo's full lips quirked slightly, knowingly. Mockingly, she thought, and frowned.

She did not understand the tension that rolled through the room, seeming to rebound off of the elegant wall-hangings. She told herself it was no more complicated than his sudden return, his unexpected appearance before her.

The castello had been a very different place while he'd been gone. She could remember what it had been like before, every time Leo had left on another one of his business trips. He had gone to Bangkok, New York, Tokyo, Singapore—and she had been trapped.

In retrospect, it was so easy to see how well the cousins had played on her fears. While Leo had been in residence, they'd been nothing but charming—yet once he'd left, they'd attacked. But this time the castello had been empty of their negative voices.

Bethany had been able to wander through it at her leisure, with no one whispering poison in her ear or pointing out her unsuitability at every turn. It was as if she'd come to the place brand new. As if it were scrubbed free of ghosts.

She had not cared for the softening she had felt as she moved through the place, exploring it as if it were a beloved museum of a house she'd once known, a home. As if, given the opportunity, she could truly fall in love with it as she had when she'd first laid eyes on it so long ago.

She did not feel so differently about the man, she thought as she studied him now, and that shook her, down to her bones and back again. Her frown deepened, even as her heart began to pound.

"You look as if you have seen a ghost," he said with his usual inconvenient perceptiveness. Bethany actually smiled then, very nearly amused at her own predictability where this man was concerned, but covered it by leaning down and reaching for her book.

"Quite the opposite," she murmured.

She straightened and pushed her curls back from her face with one hand. She wished she had tamed the great mess of them into an elegant chignon or a sleek bun. She wished she had it in her to be appropriate. But then, she reminded herself, she had no need to seek his approval any longer. She told herself she did not want to, in any event, no matter the quickening in her pulse.

She placed the book next to her on the settee, and took her time about looking up at him again. "I hope you have come to tell me it is time to visit the divorce court?"

His expression darkened. He was still propped up against the doorjamb, yet somehow he had taken over the whole of the small room in that way of his, using up all the air, stealing all the light.

"I am afraid not," he drawled. There was something she couldn't quite understand in his tone, something she did not want to comprehend in his gaze. "Though your impatience is duly noted."

"I have been here for days and days," she pointed out mildly enough. "I did not ask you to travel half the world away. Once again, I must remind you that I have an entire life in Toronto—"

"You do not need to remind me, Bethany," he interrupted silkily, her name like some kind of incantation on his lips. She shivered involuntarily. His gaze slammed into hers. "I think of your lover often. It is a subject I find unaccountably captivating."

Her breath deserted her then, and she realized that she had actually forgotten all about that seemingly harmless lie. She wrenched her gaze away from his and contemplated her hands for one moment, then another, while she attempted to remain calm. Why did she have the near-overwhelming urge to confess the truth to him? Did she really believe that would change anything?

"My lover," she repeated.

"Of course," Leo said, his gaze never leaving

her face. "We must make sure we do not forget him in all of this."

She fought off the flush of temper that colored her face. None of that mattered now. And she knew why he pretended to care about any lover she might have taken—he sought to own her, to control her, because she bore his name. It was about his reputation. His honor. Him—and that damned Di Marco legacy that he saw as being the most important part of himself.

"I am surprised that you have taken the news of him so…easily," she said, holding herself too still. "I rather thought you would have a different reaction."

"The fact that you have taken a lover, Bethany, is a grave and deep insult to my honor and to my name," Leo said softly, a thundercloud in his coffee eyes—confirming her own conclusions that simply. But then his brows rose. "But, since you are in such a great hurry to divest yourself of that name, thus removing the stain upon the Di Marco name, why should I object?"

She stared at him, a mix of despair and fury swirling in her belly, making her flush red. He would never, ever change. He could not change. She even understood that salient truth differently now, having had these past days to really investigate the mausoleum where he'd been raised, and having finally, belatedly understood the kind of life he must have led.

He had been carefully cultivated his whole life to be exactly who he was. He'd been educated, molded, primed and prepared to assume his title, his wealth, his lands and his many business concerns. She was the idiot for having ever expected something different.

And if his belief that she could have betrayed him would help her gain her freedom, that was what she wanted. What she needed. She did not really believe that she could hurt him—that it was possible to hurt him. She told herself the softening she felt inside, the longing to explain herself, was no more than a distraction. She took a deep breath and refused to allow herself that distraction.

"What is your excuse this time?" she asked finally.

She raised her gaze to his and was surprised at the expression she found there. Not the fury she might have expected. Something softer, more considering. More dangerous. Her pulse skipped, then took on a staccato beat.

"For not going to court immediately?" she hastened to add.

He shrugged, a wonderfully unconcerned Italian gesture that should not have warmed her as it did. What was the matter with her? Their most recent parting had been bleak, and yet she practically fell at his feet simply because he'd bothered to return?

She was aghast at her own weakness. Her susceptibility. She knew that his vow to keep from touching her was a godsend. It might very well be the only thing that saved her from herself.

"It is Friday afternoon," he said. When she stared at him blankly, he laughed. "The court is not open on the weekend, Bethany. And Monday is a holiday. I am afraid you must suffer through a few more days as my wife."

She could not understand the undercurrents that swirled between them then. It was as if he'd changed somehow, as if everything had changed without her noticing it—but why should it have? She remembered his bitter expression in the breakfast room, the things he'd said, the same old cycle of their frustrating conversation. Blame, recrimination and that ever-tightening noose of shame and hurt she carried inside of her, made all the more acute when she was with him.

She'd had days to ponder the whole of that interaction, and had come away none the wiser. Yet somehow she was even further determined to simply put an end to the back and forth.

What was the point of it, when it got them nowhere, when it only made her feel worse?

He moved farther into the room and Bethany had to fight the urge to rise to her feet, to face him on a more equal physical level. The room was too small, she told herself, and he too easily dominated it. That did not mean he dominated her. She would not let it. She would not let him.

"Have you ever wondered what would happen if I did not, as you say, keep you in a box?" he asked, his voice so smooth, so quiet, it washed through her like wine. Like heat. It took her too long to make sense of what he'd said. She blinked. If he had produced a second head from the back of his sweater and begun speaking with it, Bethany could not have been more surprised.

"Of course I have," she said, too shocked to be careful. "Just as I wonder what the world would be like if Santa Claus were real, or if all manner of magical creatures walked among us."

He did not take the bait. His inky dark brows rose, daring her, and she felt herself flush. Then, unaccountably, an edgy kind of anger swept through her, cramping her belly and making her pulse pound.

"I am not going to play games with you,

Leo," she said stiffly, a sudden, terrific storm swirling inside of her, clouds and panic and thunder. She shot to her feet and found her hands in tight fists at her sides. "I am not going to have fairy tale conversations with you, or salt the wounds with discussions of 'what if.'"

"Coward."

It was such a little word, said so softly, almost kindly—yet it set Bethany ablaze. She felt the kick of her temper like a wildfire and clamped down on it desperately. She would not implode. She would not give him the satisfaction of making her do so. She would not crack, not now, not after she had worked so hard to remain calm and cool around him. She only glared at him mutinously.

"You are a coward," he repeated with a gleam in his eyes that she could not mistake for anything save what it was: satisfaction. That he was getting to her. That he could poke at her. He was not the only one with the ability to read things he should not be able to see. "You have complained at length that I did this thing to you, that I insisted upon it—but, when I ask you to imagine what it might be like if I did not, you lose your temper. You cannot even have the conversation. What are you afraid of?"

"I do not see the point of hypothetical discussions," she said as icily as she could.

She recognized on some dim level that she wanted to scream. To let everything out in a rush, like a tidal wave. But why should she feel this way? Surely there were any number of things that he'd already said to her that were far, far worse than this game he suddenly wanted to play.

"Then by all means let us not dwell in hypotheticals," he said smoothly—almost, she thought with sudden suspicion, as if he had planned this. He opened up his hands and spread them wide, as if between them he held all the world. "Consider yourself out of the box, Bethany. What happens now?"

She knew then, with shattering insight, why her reaction was this unwieldy surge of rage, this piping-hot furnace of anger—it covered up the dangerous longing beneath. The quicksand of her long-lost dreams, her once-upon-a-time, naïve wishes, the epic and impossible hopes she'd pinned on this frustrating man. Her prince.

For a long moment she felt suspended in his knowing gaze, lost in it, as if he was truly offering her the things she was afraid to admit she still wanted.

Wanted once, she amended quickly, but no more. I want nothing from him any longer—this is only a memory. Just a game. It's not real.

It could not be real. What she felt as she stared at him was an echo, surely? Nothing more.

"Why would you want to do this?" she heard herself ask as if from afar. As if someone else had said it.

The drawing room, with its scarlets and golds, its exquisitely crafted furniture and graceful wall-hangings, disappeared. She could not feel the floor beneath her bare feet. She could not see anything but his fierce, focused gaze. There was only Leo and the vast sea of things she wanted from him that she could never, ever have.

"Why not?" he asked in the same tone, as if they stood together, yet still not touching, on the edge of a vast precipice and below them was nothing but darkness and turmoil. "What is left for us to lose?"

Bethany understood in that moment that she was every bit the coward that he had called her, and it galled her. Deeply. She felt her temper dissipate as if it had never been, leaving her slightly nauseated in its aftermath. But she took a deep breath, blinked away the sheen of anger and panicked temper in her eyes and confronted the facts. They were steadying, somehow, for all she would have preferred to ignore them.

There was truly nothing left to lose here, just

as he'd said. So why was she so determined to protect herself? Why did she imagine her girlish, silly fantasies about who they could have been would matter once these strange in-between days were finished? Why did she act as if it would kill her to let him know how much she had once wanted him, and how desperately?

None of this had killed her yet, after all, and she had spent long nights wishing it would, hoping it would, so she would no longer have to live like such a broken, ruined thing. So she would not have to face herself and figure out how to survive him. The likelihood was that she would live through this, however unpleasant the process might be. And if that was the case why should she keep up the fruitless pretenses that had never protected her from him in the first place?

What did she have left except the truth, no matter how unvarnished?

"I cannot bear it if you use this as one more weapon against me," she said, feeling stripped and naked in a way she never had before, not even in the worst ugliness of their previous battles. Her hands fell, empty, against her thighs. "I cannot bear it if you mock this too."

His dark eyes glittered with something heavy and intense, but he did not look away. She respected him more, perhaps, because he did not rush to give her assurances she would have questioned anyway. She did not know why she trusted him more in this strange, bare moment than she ever had before. She did not know why it mattered, but it did. Something hard and bright kindled to life in her broken, battered heart, though she refused to look at it closely.

"I cannot promise you anything," he said after a long moment, still looking at her as if she was made of glass that only he could see through. "But I can try."

Bare feet and a picnic basket, of all things.

Those were her first two demands the following morning when she met him at breakfast with a sparkle in her bright summer eyes. Leo had not seen her eyes dance like that, merry and mischievous, in far too long. He did not wish to speculate about the surprising depth of his own reaction.

"I beg your pardon?" he asked, but he was only feigning his customary hauteur. She smiled, that lush mouth curving in a way that sent heat straight to his head, his groin. Oh, the ways he wanted her. But he could not take her as he yearned to do. He could only wait, though it rankled more with each passing second. "You wish for me to scrabble around in the dirt?"

"Like the common peasant you will never, ever be," she confirmed with no little satisfaction and arched her fine, dark brows challengingly when he laughed.

"And just like that a lifetime of assumptions about the fairer sex disappears into the ether," he said dryly. He let his eyes trace a longing pattern along her delicate neck, deep into the shadow between the breasts her blouse concealed. His fingers twitched with the need to touch her, to suit action to yearning, but he shoved it aside. "One would think they'd all prefer the prince to the frog, but not you, Bethany. Of course not you."

His words sat there between them on the gleaming breakfast table, shining in the morning light, weaving in between the platters of food and carafes of steaming coffee, hot tea, and freshly squeezed juices. He had meant them playfully enough, but her expression changed, becoming more guarded as she gazed at him. She cleared her throat and shifted slightly in her chair.

"There is no point playing these games," she said, her voice stiffer than it had been before. And, he thought, far sadder. He wished he did not feel both as a personal loss. "I don't know why we are bothering. Nothing will change the facts of our situation."

"Indeed, nothing will," he agreed, aware that he and she had very different ideas about what those facts entailed. But this was not the time to explore those differences. This was no time to feel.

What was the matter with him? This entire situation was about the fulfillment of obligations—hers. He did not know why he was entertaining her requests, worrying about whether or not he had treated her fairly. It did not signify; no matter how she had been treated, it was time to take her rightful place at his side. He was not a man who failed twice and, having accepted his first failure, he knew he would not repeat it. He should not allow anything else to keep him from securing her—or, at the very least, explaining to her exactly what he planned.

Annoyed with himself, and his own inability to say what he should, he rose and headed toward the door.

"Where are you going?" she asked. He was sure it said things about him he was better off not examining that he was pleased to hear the uncertainty in her voice.

Why should he be the only one left unsettled by these seething, unmanageable, unspoken issues that swirled between them, making every moment fraught with tension? History?

Longing? Perhaps that was why he did not call this ill-conceived game of hers to a halt. Perhaps that was why he continued to indulge her.

He turned at the door and let his gaze fall on her. She was so artlessly beautiful, this faithless wife of his, with the light streaming in to light up her face, make a symphony of her glorious eyes and wash her dark curls with gold. He had never been able to control this need for her that ravaged through him, that compelled him, that never, ever left him.

She bit at her lower lip, and he felt it as if she'd sunk those white teeth into his own flesh. He wanted to taste her more than he could remember wanting anything else. But first he was going to play this game of hers. And he was going to win it.

Then, perhaps, they could compare their facts and discuss a few home truths he was certain she would not like at all.

Leo shoved the burning desire as far down as he could and forced himself to look at her blandly, politely. As if he could not imagine six separate ways to take her right here, right now. On the table, on the floor, up against the windows with the light bathing them in—

But that was not productive.

"I must have my valet prepare the appropriate

attire to complement bare feet," he said instead, lazily.

He gazed at her until her neck washed red, and then he smiled, because he knew exactly how she felt. Winded. Hungry. And resentful of both.

This was about crawling out of boxes and removing boundaries, Bethany reminded herself, and that was why she pushed her way into Leo's bedchamber not long after he'd disappeared into it.

He had never encouraged her to treat his chamber as her own, unless they were naked. And she had heard more than enough from his cousin Vincentio on the topic of appropriate behavior for the wife of such an important man as the *Principe di Felici*, so she had not attempted it.

She shook off the past with effort and stepped into the principe's master suite.

It befitted the noble ruler of an ancient line. It was magnificent and profoundly male. Deep reds and lustrous mahoganies dominated the great room and the four-poster bed that rose in the center like an altar.

Bethany's throat went dry, and she found herself wringing her hands like some kind of virgin sacrifice before she caught herself and stopped.

The rugs at her feet were old, impressive. They whispered of wealth across the centuries, of ancient trading routes and princes long past whose regal feet had stepped where hers did now. She wished for a moment that Leo could be just a man, just the simple man she had imagined him to be when she'd first met him in the Hawaiian surf. But even as she wished it something in her rejected the thought.

He had called himself 'unintelligible' without his family's history, and the truth was she could not imagine him separate from all that sweeping past entailed. As awe-inspiring as even his bedchamber might be, a paean to Renaissance architecture and aesthetics, she could not deny that it suited him. He was every inch a prince. He always had been.

Then he walked into the room and Bethany froze.

Her breath caught in her throat and her knees felt like water. He was wearing clothes that Bethany would have sworn this man did not own. On some level, perhaps, she had imagined that her request for bare feet and casual clothing would catch him out—would force him into some kind of awkwardness, make him something more normal, more ordinary.

She should have known better. She should not have forgotten.

Leo sauntered toward her, his eyes hard on hers, alive with a glittering heat that made her body shake with helpless response. Her nipples hardened against her soft cotton shirt, while everywhere else she melted.

He wore a pair of low-slung, faded denim jeans that clung to his mouthwatering form in a way that made her feel light-headed. And he wore nothing on his magnificent torso save one very, very tight black T-shirt.

Even dressed like the simple man of her old fantasies, Leo Di Marco was completely and totally at ease, fully in command.

It was impossible to drag her eyes away from his toned and rangy body, especially when he moved. His smile was sharp, hungry, his eyes all-seeing, all-knowing. Bethany realized at once that, as ever with this man, she had miscalculated.

She had forgotten how lethal Leo was, how elemental.

If anything, the sleek business suits and predictable finery of the *Principe di Felici* distracted from Leo's essential male charisma, no doubt allowing him to do business without sending all those around him into fits of the vapors.

How could she have forgotten what lay beneath?

This was the man who had swept her off of her feet, altering her life completely with one slow smile. *This* was the man she had seen in the warm, soft waters of Waikiki, this confident and dangerously attractive man, all hot eyes and a hard body, who had shorted out her mind, her body, her heart.

This stripped-down, lean and hungry creature was the one she had followed all the way to Italy. *This* was the man she had married and had loved with every fiber of her being, only to see him swallowed whole into the great, vast mouth of his family, his history, his endless obligations.

The last time she had seen this man, he had convinced her over the course of two heady, passion-drenched, impossible weeks to turn her back on everything she had ever known, marry a stranger and ride off into a sunset she had trusted him to provide.

What would he do this time? When she knew better and still, her heart stopped at the sight of all that casual, male grace? When she hadn't managed a full breath since he'd walked through that door?

This was not a game at all, Bethany realized, far too late, astounded at the breadth of her own stupidity—her own great weakness. This was everything she'd lost. This was everything she grieved for.

This was a huge mistake.

CHAPTER NINE

"You have been at pains to tell me what you are not," he said in that rich, low voice that for all its gentleness still seemed to Bethany to take over the whole of the Felici Valley. "Perhaps it is time to tell me who you are."

They walked along the cypress-studded footpath that wound down from the castello toward the valley floor and which would, Leo had promised, lead them to a secluded lake just over the crest of the next hill.

It was like a dream, Bethany thought, feeling as if she watched them from some distance— as if that was not her who walked on a warm autumn morning with this dark, brooding, impossibly handsome man, but some other woman. One who was not afraid that her slightest move might shatter this unexpected, fragile accord. One who knew nothing of the long war that had come before and scarred them both.

Oh, the people they could have been. The

people they should have been! Bethany could feel the bite of that loss, that tragedy, all around her in the air like the hint of a changing season.

Or perhaps it was simply that they were free of the castello today, free of its heavy stone walls and the great weight of its history—free of the people they had to be when they were inside it.

She darted a glance at him, at his high cheekbones and flashing eyes, at that satyr's mouth that had once felt so decadent against her skin, yet could flatten into such a grim and disapproving line when he was disappointed with her. And he had so often been disappointed in her.

Next to her, his long legs keeping pace with her shorter ones with no apparent effort, he swung the basket laden with delicacies from the kitchens in one large hand. He seemed as easy with his bare feet stuck in the dirt of his family's land as he did in full princely regalia at the head of the massive banquet table in the castello's great hall. For some reason, that observation made her heart seem to expand inside her chest, almost to the point of pain.

"You finished a degree at university, I believe?" he prompted her when it became clear that she was not going to speak of her own volition. Bethany laughed slightly, flustered.

"Yes," she said, struggling to collect herself, to cast aside the enchantment of the countryside, so green and gold and inviting in the sunshine with the great expanse of the cerulean sky arched above them. To forget what had not been, and could not be. "I studied psychology."

To find out what was so terribly wrong with me that I could disappear so fully into you, she thought, but did not say. As if I'd never existed at all.

"Fascinating," he murmured, and though she shot a sharp look at him his expression was mild. "I had no idea the human mind was of such interest to you."

Only yours, she thought with some fatalism, but then pulled herself together. That was not entirely true, in any case, and this was a day without lies or pretense, she decided. She could act as if they were suspended out of time, as if they had escaped their history today, their tangled and heavy past.

"Human interaction interests me," she said. "My mother was an archaeologist, which is something similar, I suppose. She wanted to figure out human lives from the things left behind in ruins. I am less interested in the remains of societies and more interested in how people survive what occurs in their own lives."

She thought that was too much, that she'd

gone too far, revealed herself. She pulled her lower lip between her teeth as she waited for an explosion, a reaction. Leo shot a dark, unreadable look at her, from beneath lashes that were frankly unfair on a man of his physical size and indisputable prowess, but did not strike back as she'd expected.

"You do not normally speak of your mother," he said. Did she only imagine his hesitant tone? Was he as loath to disrupt this fragile peace as she was?

"She died when I was still so young, just a baby," she said. She shrugged, wrinkling her nose up toward the sun, tilting her head back to let the warm rays caress her face. "To be honest, I cannot remember her at all." His silence, his somehow comforting presence beside her, encouraged her to continue. "My father never spoke of her when I was growing up. I think it caused him too much pain. But then toward the end he could not seem to speak of anything else."

She looked down at her feet, slightly chilled against the rich earth, but it felt good to be barefoot, to act as if she was free of cares, regardless of the truth. "I think he was afraid that if he did not she would disappear when he did."

The path along the valley floor meandered through the vineyards before beginning an easy climb toward the next rolling hill. They walked side by side, as if they had all the time in the world, Bethany thought. As if they were under enchantment. As if this game of theirs was real and they could live this day forever.

What did it say about her that so much of her wished that they could?

"When I returned to Toronto…" she began, sneaking a look at him and flushing slightly when he met her gaze, his eyes sardonic. "I wanted to finish my degree," she continued hurriedly, jerking her gaze away. "And I suppose in some way I wanted to honor her, too. It felt like a continuation of her studies, somehow."

"I am glad for you," he said simply when she stopped talking and returned her attention to the path in front of them. "I know you wanted very much to maintain ties with your family however you could."

She did not like the way he said that—as if he had spent time pondering her. As if he knew things about her that she might not, as if he cared in ways she was not prepared to accept. It made her feel restless in a way she could not name.

"That cannot be something you ever worry about," she said, changing the focus of this odd, out-of-body conversation, pushing the spotlight away from herself and the panic that she desperately wanted to hide. "You cannot take a step without coming face to face with the Di Marco history."

He smiled slightly.

"Indeed I cannot," he agreed. "But it is not necessarily the voyage of discovery you seem to imagine, I think." He let out a short laugh. "My father was not an easy man. He believed absolutely in his own dominion over all things. His wealth and estates. His wife and family. He was neither tolerant nor kind."

"Leo…" But he did not hear her, or he did not choose to stop.

"I was sent to boarding school in Austria when I was barely turned four," Leo said in that same matter-of-fact, emotionless voice. "It was a slightly more nurturing environment than my father's home. I was raised to think that nothing and no one could ever be as important as the Di Marco legacy. My responsibilities and obligations were beaten into me early." His eyes met hers, and she could not read what swam in those bittersweet, chocolate depths, just as she could not identify the mess of emotion that fought inside of her. "There is a certain liberty in having no choices, you must understand."

"That sounds horrible," she said, her eyes heavy with tears she could not shed where he could see her. "Cancer took my mother too soon, and my father grieved for her the rest of his days, but he loved me. I never doubted that he loved me."

"I was raised to disdain such foolishness," Leo said, something indefinable across that mobile, fascinating face before he hid it behind his customary mask of polite indifference.

She knew she should recognize that odd expression—that something in her swelled to meet it, to match it—but her mind shied away from it before she could properly identify it. She found she was holding her breath.

"The Di Marcos, no doubt, had more important things to concentrate on," she managed to say, forcing herself to breathe past the knot in her belly.

"My duties were very clear from a very young age, and there was never any point in rebelling or arguing," he continued, his voice hushed, his eyes clear. "I must never forget myself and act with the recklessness of other young men. I must always think of the Di Marco legacy first, never my own needs or desires." He shrugged. "If I forgot myself, there were never any shortage of people around to remind me. Especially my father, using any means he deemed necessary."

"That seems so cruel." Bethany could not

look at him; she was afraid she would try to do something she should not, like hold him, or soothe him, or try to make something up to the little boy she was not certain he had ever been. "You were a child, not a tiny robot to be programmed according to a set of archaic demands!"

"My father did not want a child," Leo said quietly. "He wanted the next *Principe di Felici.*"

There did not seem to be anything she could say to such a simple yet devastating statement. It hung there with them, as if it ripened on the vines that stretched out beside them and climbed the hill along with them.

Bethany could not bring herself to speak because she was afraid the tears she fought to keep at bay would spill over and betray her, and the worst of it was, she was not entirely certain what emotions these were that held her so securely in a tight, fast grip. She only knew that things were clear to her now that had not been clear before, though she could not have articulated what she meant by that.

She only knew the truth of it, and that that truth was painful and seared her right through to the bone.

But then they reached the top of the second hill and her breath caught in her throat for an entirely different reason. The path delivered them to the banks of an absolutely perfect, kidney-shaped lake. The water gleamed like crystal and glass in the autumn sun, basking in the late-morning light. All around, birds called from the shade trees, and sweet-smelling grass swept along the banks.

"This is beautiful," Bethany breathed. But a different set of tears stung her eyes now. How could she have missed this place, in a year and a half spent only a hill away? How was that possible? She had the strangest sense of vertigo—as if everything she had accepted as fact, had acted upon, was spun around before her, out of focus and somehow not at all what she had believed it to be.

"My mother might have been an artist," Leo said in that low, irresistible voice of his, velvet and steel, whiskey and chocolate. He gazed out over the postcard-perfect setting, though the look in his eyes was far away. "Had she not had the misfortune to be the *Principessa di Felici*. When she provided my father with the necessary heir, he provided her with a token of appreciation for services rendered. This lake."

He crossed his arms over his leanly muscled chest, making the black T-shirt strain against his well-formed biceps.

"He had it made to resemble a lake on an estate in Andalucia where my mother spent summers as a girl." He sent her a dark look beneath a sardonic lift of his brow. "But do not cast my father as a romantic in this scenario. He had not one sensitive bone in his body. He did, however, care deeply about public opinion, and the birth of a new prince was certainly an event worth celebrating in an ostentatious manner."

He waved a hand at the enchanting, peaceful view. "And he built her a lake so that forever after Domenico Di Marco might be hailed as the great romantic hero he was not."

"It is beautiful," Bethany said again, more firmly, past the lump in her throat, the ache in her heart. "However it came to be here."

She moved toward the water, that same deep restlessness making her feel edgy, nervous. She stared out over the sparkling surface for long moments, only half-aware that he was moving around behind her. She needed to think, to calm herself. She needed to rein in the wild, chaotic emotions that buffeted her. This was supposed to be a different kind of day—no wildness, no upset.

Surely she could handle that? Surely she could manage to keep her cool if Leo, of all people, could bring himself to talk to her like this?

She would not let herself regret that it could happen only now, when it was all over between them save the legalities. She would not imagine what might have been between them if this day had occurred three years ago, four years ago, instead of now. She would not ruin this, whatever it was, with the things that could not be changed no matter how this day went. No matter what she felt.

When she turned back around, he had set out a large, square ground-covering and had unpacked some of the hamper's tempting items. Cold chicken, a bowl of olives. Wine and two glasses. Cheeses and slices of meats—*carpaccio, prosciutto*—and a selection of pâtés. Slices of apple and plump bunches of grapes.

He lounged across the blue and white blanket, his jeans-clad body on deliberate display, every inch of him clearly a delectable and dangerous male animal, for all that he appeared so indolent. She could not seem to look at that tight black T-shirt without losing her focus, much less the tanned, taut ridge of his abdomen that was revealed beneath the hiked-up hem. She had to swallow twice.

The look in his dark eyes, when they met hers, made her temperature soar. She felt feverish, too hot and too cold all at the same time.

"Come sit with me," he said, the wolf to the foolish girl.

And, because she had never been anything

but a fool when she was near him, no matter what else she might have been or wanted to be, she did.

Bethany knew the moment she lowered herself to the ground beside him that something had changed. She wanted it to be no more than a shift in the light breeze that danced in the trees above her head, or in the temperature of the day around them, but she was afraid she knew better.

She tucked the white cotton skirt she'd worn because it felt far too casual for a *principessa* tight around her knees, and tried to keep her attention trained on the beautiful water in front of her rather than the raw sexual energy emanating from the man lounging next to her.

"Are you not hungry?" he asked after one heated moment bled into another. She could not help herself—she turned to look at him, as if his very body commanded her and she was helpless to do anything but obey.

And he knew it. She could see that smug, male satisfaction in his dark gaze, the faint smile that toyed with the corner of his mouth.

She did not know what to do. She knew how she might have handled this moment even two hours ago, but that had been before they'd walked through fields of green and gold and he'd told her things that still made her feel raw. Unsettled.

That had been before her traitorous heart had let itself yearn for him so fully, as completely as if he had never broken it in the first place. What was she supposed to do now?

"How did your meetings in Sydney go?" she asked, because it seemed so innocuous a question and because it could not possibly make this tension between them any worse. And perhaps because she was every bit the coward he had called her.

Leo's smile deepened, and he reached down to capture a piece of hard cheese with his long fingers. He took a bite, considering her, and she could not have said why she found all of it unbearably erotic.

The lake was so quiet, the breeze so sweet against her skin. The sun above them was so warm, caressing. Her breasts felt heavy, aching behind her thin shirt. She felt a faint sheen of moisture break out across her upper lip.

She knew he missed nothing. His head cocked to the side. "I do not often lose the things I want, Bethany. But perhaps you knew this already."

"I know you take your business very seriously, if that is what you mean," she said, unable to look away from the dark seduction of his gaze, unable to keep herself from imagining what might happen if she tilted forward and let herself fall across that hard, rangy body spread out before her like a buffet of sensual delights.

But of course she already knew what would happen. She could already taste the salt and musk of his skin against her tongue. She could already feel his long, smooth muscles hard beneath her palms. She could hardly breathe for the images that chased through her head, memory and imagination fused into one great wave of ache and want and need.

She knew that he knew it, too.

"I take everything seriously," he said, his voice a low rumble she could feel as well as hear, moving through her, leaving heat and fire in its wake. "I am known for my attention to detail. Renowned for it, you might even say."

"Leo…" She did not know what she meant to say, but she felt so snared, so captured, as if he'd trapped her here. The truly terrifying part of that was how little she cared. What was happening to her? How could she let him cast this spell over her just by lying there?

But she had the lowering thought that she'd left the fight somewhere back at the castello. That he had finally disarmed her and she was more vulnerable now than she had ever been before. Mostly because she could not bring herself to care as she knew she had even this morning. As she knew she would again when this dangerous moment was past.

Still, here—now—there was only his hot gaze and her helpless melting deep within.

"I can see the way you look at me, Bethany," he whispered, his eyes intent on hers, his voice a seduction, a caress. "You are eating me alive with all that blue heat, all of your desires written like poetry across your face. I can see that your breathing has gone shallow and your hands tremble."

"Perhaps this is disgust," she breathed. "After all."

He smiled, but it was a predator's smile, and it connected hard with her core, sending heat searing through her. Electric. Shattering. Leo.

"You are the student of psychology," he said. "You tell me what it means, these physical signs and your continued denials that they mean what we both know they must mean."

Bethany looked away then, the word 'psychology' managing to break through the haze. *You have another life, a different life,* she told herself fiercely, trying to breathe through the tightness inside of her that mounted with every beat of her heart. *This is just a dream by a lake that should not exist in the first place.*

"I do not need to be a psychologist to know

that touching you would be a monumentally stupid thing to do," she said in a low voice, her attention trained on the lake's clear waters as they lapped against the shore.

"If you say so," he murmured, sounding neither offended nor put off. Hyper-aware of him, she could practically hear every shift of his body.

She knew when he reached for the succulent cuts of salami and prosciutto crudo, when he tore off a piece of fresh-baked bread and slathered it with an olive tapenade. She knew when he relaxed back on his elbows, when he licked his fingers, when he let that hungry gaze of his eat her up instead.

"Why did you never bring me here?" she asked finally when she could no longer stare at the lake without driving herself insane.

Was it worse to imagine what he was doing or watch him do it? All these years later, and she still did not know. She twisted around to look at him, not surprised to find him watching her with that same intense regard.

"Before," she amended.

He looked at her for a moment, then out toward the opposite bank of the lake where leafy green persimmon trees rustled in the slight breeze.

"This was never a happy place," he said finally. "It did not seem appropriate to bring a new bride to a place made from one man's ego and a woman's tears."

Bethany swallowed. "And now?"

Why did she ask? What did she want from him?

But she knew what she wanted. She had always known: everything. That was why the little she'd received had hurt so very badly. That was why she had haunted that house in Toronto for so long, hoping in the dark of night that he might return even as she hated herself for that weakness in the light of day.

She was merely feeling the echoes of all of that now, she told herself desperately. Just the echoes, nothing more.

"What answer do you wish me to give?" he asked softly, turning that brooding yet fierce gaze back upon her. "What must I tell you to make you touch me as you want to do, Bethany? As we both want you to do? Tell me what you want and I will say it. Just tell me."

It was as if there was a sudden earthquake beneath her—as if the earth tumbled and rolled, cracked and heaved all while she sat there, not moving, not touching him, not even fighting with him—which was, she acknowledged in some far-off part of her brain, far easier than whatever this was.

This…aching regret. This longing. This undeniable need and this deep, wrenching fear that if she did not reach over and place her hands on him he would truly disappear as if he had never been.

Because he never should have been. He never should have noticed her in the first place. He had never been meant for her—he had always been on loan, and some part of her had recognized that from the start.

Was that why she had thrown tantrums, indulged her inner lunatic, done everything possible to push him away? Had she done it all to hasten along the inevitable day when he looked at her and saw nothing but his worst mistake? Why not rush to that end, when she'd known they were always destined to get there one way or another?

"You look at me as if I have become a ghost," he said, his eyes narrowing. "Before your very eyes."

"Sometimes I think that's all you ever were," she heard herself say as if she had no control over herself any longer—as if all the things she had only ever admitted to herself in the dark of the night were suddenly free to tumble from her lips. As if this secluded, unnatural spot, so pretty and so calculated at the same time, was somehow the safe haven she had searched for all these years.

"That is all you allowed me to be," he said quietly. "It is all you would give me—your body, your protestations of love. But the real woman? The flesh and blood? That was never on offer."

Any other day she might have thrown something back at him, tried to hurt him in return. But today was too different. Too out of time, as if their usual rules did not apply. Or perhaps it was this odd place, this peaceful lake hidden away on a hilltop, yet never meant for happiness—just like us, she thought.

She could not bring herself to do anything but reply honestly.

"Whose flesh and blood did you want?" she asked, her voice as soft as his. "You wanted something I could never be. You wanted the woman you should have married. The woman you would have married, had you not met me instead."

She did not know what she expected from him. Protestations? Denials? Some part of her yearned for him to storm at her that she was mistaken, to demand that she tell him who had put such thoughts in her head. But he did neither.

Instead, his dark gaze seemed electric on

hers, searing and hard, and his face darkened. A moment passed, and then another, and he did not speak.

"You were meant for someone noble, well-educated, refined and elegant," she continued, reciting from memory the words his cousin had hurled at her, trapped in Leo's gaze but unable to look away. "Every day I was none of those things, and every day you resented me more for it."

"No," he said, his eyes clear on hers even though his voice was gruff. "I did not. I did not resent you for that." He paused, then continued, his voice low and harsh. "If anything, I resented myself for trying to make you into something you were not."

She opened her mouth then, but nothing came out. She looked at him and it was as if she shook, or the earth shook, but nothing made sense. It was all a jumble of regret and mis-understanding; her own fears and his cousins' poison; his retreat into his title and her inability to reach out to him; resentment and anger, the wounds inflicted across the years, and her in-ability to dismiss him as she should. And she knew she should.

"The fact that you were not those things, could never be those things, was why I married you in the first place," he said, his voice softer, yet somehow more urgent.

She was astounded to realize that she believed him. Yet she remembered how it had been. He had been so cold, so distant, so disapproving, and she had not known how to handle that when the man she had fallen so far in love with had been so fiery, so deeply entwined with her at every moment.

"Why did you not tell me that then?" she asked, surprised to find she was whispering. Would it have made a difference? she asked herself now. Would it have changed anything?

"I could not tell you something I did not know myself," he said in a low voice.

But she could not get past what his words seemed to imply. And she was shaken by the wave of grief that washed through her, over her, making her feel too large and unwieldy, too exposed, too vulnerable.

"You wanted something different, is that it?" she asked, because she could not seem to stop herself, not because she really wanted to know the answer. Her voice was hoarse from the agony of this conversation. She was sure she had bruises, yet she still could not seem to stop. "You...what? Thought I could be the symbol of your rebellion?"

"I wanted you," he said, his voice as dark

as his eyes, his expression as troubled as she imagined hers to be. His lips pressed together and she could see that tension radiating along the length of his body. "I wanted you. And I confess, Bethany, that I did not think of anything else at all."

She wanted to weep. To curl herself into a ball and sob until the great mess of the feelings that swirled around inside of her were purged from her once and for all.

But instead, responding to an urgency she dared not examine too closely, she leaned forward. She propped herself up on her hands and held herself above him for a long, trembling moment. Then she closed the distance between them and went to press her lips to his.

"Wait."

He stopped her just before she touched him and she froze, her mouth so close to his, so very close. She dragged her gaze up to his, so bright now, with desire glowing like molten gold. She shivered and he smiled, though his whole big body was as taut as a spring, coiled tight beneath her, so much raw male power leashed and ready.

"What is it?" she whispered just a breath away. Her heart pounded wildly in her chest, and she could see his hands in fists at his hips, digging into the blue and white blanket beneath them.

"If I taste you, I will take you." His eyes, glittering with that intoxicating heat, were hard on hers. His harsh promise hung between them and lit her on fire. She exulted in the flames, the burn. "Be certain, Bethany. Be very certain."

She was not certain at all. She felt reckless, compelled. She felt as if she had lost herself in quicksand. She felt too much, all of it so big, so terrifying, shaking her even as she sat.

I wanted you, he had said, and it made her shiver. Today of all days, here beside a lake that should not have been—a monument to a marriage disturbingly like the one she had walked away from—she would not let herself worry about the consequences.

She licked her lips and felt him sigh against her, felt that dark and intoxicating desire kick hard and hot between them.

Just for today, she promised herself. This is only for today.

And then, reaching across all of their history, across too many years and regrets, too much resentment and the space of one quick breath, she fit her mouth to his.

CHAPTER TEN

LEO let her kiss him, her soft, lush mouth hot against his. Once. Twice. Like heaven, her taste. A kind of paradise, the slide of her lips on his—tasting, touching. Needing him as he needed her. If this was his rebellion, he did not know why he would ever do anything but fall.

And then he could not help the thudding, pounding, heady mix of desire and triumph, victory and relief that flooded through him. He jack-knifed forward, never taking his mouth from hers, and took her face in his hands, angling her head for a better, hotter, slicker fit.

Oh, the taste of her. It was like the finest of his wines, like the heat of the summer sun, and he had been hard for her for days. Years. He went harder still when he heard the impatient, greedy sounds she made, her mouth opening over his, her hands spearing into the thickness of his hair to hold his head close to hers.

He felt her fine cheekbones under his thumbs,

the soft swell of her cheeks. Still he tasted her, over and over, as if he could sate himself on this alone—as if he feared that should he stop, should they breathe, should they pause for even a moment, she would disappear from him all over again.

Not again, he told himself. Not now. Not while he captured her curls beneath his palms. Not while he tasted her as if he were dying of thirst and she was the coolest, sweetest, purest water he had ever known.

And then he could not think. He could not plan. He could only pull her close, crushing her breasts against the wall of his chest. But soon even that delicious pressure was not enough. Could anything be enough?

He shifted, sliding one hand down the enticing line of her spine, the other along the side of her body to trace her perfect, delectable curves—the side of her breast, the indentation of her waist, the fascinating curve of her hip.

When his hands reached the tempting swell of her bottom, he lifted her, shifting her up and toward him so she sat astride him, the heat of her nestled tight against the hardest part of him.

She gasped and pulled back, bracing her small hands against his shoulders, and for a long, fierce moment he gazed at her. Her curls tumbled around them, dark and wild, and her lips were swollen and slick from his. Her color was high and bright, and her eyes glowed like sapphires, dazed with the same dizzying, raging passion that charged through him, burning him alive.

She was the most beautiful creature he had ever beheld, like lightning and quicksilver in his arms, and she was his. She was his. She had always been his. Even when he had wanted her to be something other than she was, he had known that simple truth. Every curve, every sigh, every shiver that wracked her delicate body—all of it, all of her, was his.

Leo wanted to lick every single inch of her until she admitted the truth of it, until she screamed it, until she sobbed out his name like it was a prayer that only he could answer. And he would.

"Tell me you want me," he commanded her, his voice a stranger's, no more than a growl as his hands retraced their journey and she squirmed on his lap, rocking her core against him, making them both sigh as the fire licked through them.

"You know I do," she replied, more groan than words, her hands testing the shape of his shoulders, the corded muscles she found there, the smooth skin that stretched across his biceps.

He found her high breasts with his hands

and let them fill his palms, teased the hard nipples through her soft shirt until she rocked against him, her eyes dark with need, her breath coming in quick, shallow pants.

"Say it." It was a stark demand, a necessity for reasons he could not understand and did not care to examine.

As if she understood that on some primal level, she bent her head down and licked him, her small tongue tracing fire across the sensitive skin where his neck met his shoulder. He felt himself shudder with an elemental need as the storm within him began to howl.

"Bethany…" A warning. A plea.

"You know that I do," she whispered in his ear. "You have always known it."

He was lost. He found her mouth with his, hot and wet and perfect, as his hands worked between them. He tested her thighs beneath his palms, pushed her skirt out of the way and felt the scalding heat of her at her core. It inflamed him.

With a muttered curse, and more determination than skill, he released himself, letting his member free, proud and hard between them. Then he lifted her again, pulled her lacy panties to one side with an economy of motion and held himself perfectly still at her entrance for a breathless, shattering moment.

"Leo..." His name was a sob, a curse, a chant.

"Tell me." His voice was thick, tortured.

He could feel her heat, beckoning and promising, so close. So close. She squirmed against him, her hips wild beneath his hands. Desperate.

"I want to hear the words," he gritted out. "From your mouth. I want you to say it."

She wrapped her arms around his neck, pressing her breasts tighter against him, torturing them both. When she spoke it was as if it had been torn from her, as if she was as helpless in the face of this passion as he was, and he loved it.

How he loved it.

"I want you, Leo," she whispered, her voice broken, dazed, aching for him. He could feel it resonate in him, his chest, his head, his sex. "God, I want you."

He plunged into her, sheathing himself to the hilt, the fit tight and hot and as perfect as it had always been—like she was made for him, crafted expressly for this heat, this passion, *him*.

She shattered around him almost before he had finished that deep, perfect thrust. Her head fell back, her eyes drifted closed, her body rode his through tremor after tremor. He pulled back, shaking slightly with the effort, the control, reveling in the feel of her against him, so soft and wet where he was hard—all of it heaven and all of it his.

It was not enough. It was never enough.

But it was a start.

She could not breathe, she was in a thousand pieces, and yet he was still hot and hard inside of her.

Bethany managed somehow to pry open her eyes and found him watching her, his features tight and sensually intense as he gazed at her. She bit her lip as aftershocks rippled through her, making her nipples harden and her thighs clench.

Never breaking eye contact, he moved inside of her, guiding her over him.

She clung to his shoulders, loving the width and strength of them, letting her fingers caress the intriguing rock-hard muscle she found there. He held her hips in his capable hands and slowly, deliberately, he built the fire within her—stoking the embers, fanning the flames.

Bethany felt the tension she'd just released roar back, coiling with twice the strength inside of her. His thrusts were long, slow, deep, driving her mad with a need far greater, far more encompassing, than what had come before.

She could not think, she could only feel. His

mouth on hers, his face against her neck. Her breasts pressed against his chest, his strong arms encircling her. She was swept away in his demanding rhythm until all she could feel was his possession.

Deep. Slow. Devastating.

Her head fell back, and his mouth was like a brushfire against the sensitive skin of her neck, hot and electric.

"Do not close your eyes," he ordered her, his voice low and sensual. It vibrated against her, through her. She could feel it deep in her core, where he slid into her again and again, so hard and hot where she melted all around him. "You have been away from me for three years. Stay with me now."

She forced her eyes open and met his. She could feel the air sizzle. Dark need arced between them, filled her vision, became the world. The fires burned high within, turned white-hot, and still he continued to move so slowly, so deliberately, so surely, each thrust almost more than she could bear until the next. And the next.

He was killing her.

"Leo…" she whispered, desperate, her voice strangled and her eyes bright with heat. "Please…"

As if he'd been waiting for exactly that plea,

as if he'd planned it, he smiled and his thrusts grew faster, less measured. Wild and hot. Perfect.

"Now," he murmured, his voice a dark, deep command, and she shivered.

But that was not enough.

Leo reached between them, found the center of her with his sure fingers and then, as he licked her neck and took her mouth in a frank, carnal kiss of possession, he catapulted them both over the edge.

She came back to herself slowly, to find his mouth against the skin at her neck as she lay boneless against him, draped across him, her heart still pounding in her chest, her limbs, her ears.

He looked up as she stirred and she felt herself flush, whether from embarrassment or something far deeper, far more vulnerable, she could not say.

She opened her mouth to speak but nothing came out. He was still inside of her. She could feel the coarse material of his jeans against the sensitive skin of her inner thighs. She could feel his hard chest against her, his maleness deep within her, his strong arms all around her. There was a part of her that panicked at that stark evidence of his possession even as a darker part, a part she wished to deny even as she became aware of it, gloried in it.

If I taste you, I will take you, he had promised her.

And he had kept his promise.

"That was..." But her voice trailed away and she realized she was still spinning. From a single kiss she had not planned to give, to him buried inside of her. She had no idea at all how to make sense of what had happened.

It felt cataclysmic. Life-altering. And, then again, perhaps it was simply Leo.

"Yes?" he asked; teasing her, she thought.

There was a smile in his eyes, if not on his lips, and she could not have said why seeing it made her chest ache. She only knew that it hurt, that she hurt. She knew she desperately needed to think about everything that had just happened in a critical, logical, unemotional way—which was unlikely to occur while they were joined like this, in the middle of the day, outside where anyone at all could happen by and see them on the banks of a lake that should never have been made in the first place.

Her discomfort grew, skittered through her, made her stomach clench and her breath come faster.

He only gazed at her, those eyes clear in a way that made her want to pull away, shield her own eyes, hide from him. But she could hardly do such a thing in this exposed position, so she was forced to simply gaze back at him, feeling that itchy flush work its way over her skin, her discomfort made real and red on her flesh.

She felt him move slightly, deep within her, and realized with a kind of amazement that he was becoming aroused. Again.

"But you…" Her voice was too high, too breathless, as if she was someone else. She felt like someone else, someone she was not at all sure she should permit herself to acknowledge, much less embody. Someone as silly and as profoundly thrown by him as she had once been, years before. "How can you…so soon?"

He laughed then, his hands moving along her back as if he was soothing her, settling her, using his touch to calm her. She had a vague memory of him doing this long ago, gentling her with that tremendous power he unleashed only when he chose to share it. She had thought it patronizing then; she had believed it an attempt to control her.

She wished she could summon the anger that had once stirred in her, but she could feel only her body's helpless response to him, as if it wanted him in ways she was afraid to face. She wanted to shake off his hands, but she was too captivated by his expression to do more than shift against him.

And of course, when she moved, she felt him—hard and hot so deep inside of her—and she felt her own melting, shivering response.

"That was but a taste," he said, that near-smile flirting with his mouth. "It has been a long time."

Her head spun, and then the world spun too as he swung her around, moving her with an effortless might and grace, rolling them both over on the blanket. He settled himself between her thighs and looked down into her face.

He never broke their intimate connection, and she told herself that was what made her heart hammer even harder against her ribs.

"Since me, you mean?" she stammered, gazing up at him, her eyes wide with a kind of desperation.

Why did she feel the overpowering need to run from him, to put any distance between them she could? But he was everywhere—inside her, above her—and there was no escape.

"You don't mean a long time over all—you mean since me? Since you and I...?" Her voice trailed away.

The laughter faded from his expression, and an enigmatic light gleamed in his dark eyes. She shivered, and he was still inside her, growing harder by the moment. She shifted, but it only drew him in deeper, closer, and she caught her breath as sensation arrowed through her, bathing her in heat and light.

"I mean that it has been a long time since I touched you," he said, his eyes pinning her to the ground as surely as his body did, offering no quarter, no compromise. "Which also means that it has been a long time since I have touched anyone." His eyes rose, challenging her. Shaming her. Reading her secrets and laying her bare. "I take my vows very seriously, Bethany. I did not break them."

Bethany felt dizzy. Her heart fluttered wildly in her chest and she thought—she hoped—she might faint. But instead one moment dragged into another, and he simply waited. Watched and waited, when she wanted to thrash and scream and howl out her reaction, no matter how little sense that might make.

She felt lost to herself. A stranger.

"Leo..." She could only whisper his name. She could not identify the emotions that swelled in her, rolling and pitching as if she were a tiny boat adrift in a great sea. "You should know...I mean, I never..."

Who had she become? she wondered in a mix of shame, panic and something else, something far deeper and more dangerous. She could not make it through a single sentence.

She felt her eyes fill and was horrified to think she might weep. Not now. Please, not now!

Still, Leo merely waited. He only watched her, propped up on his elbows, his expression unreadable, though she could feel the great, humming power of him as if he connected her to some immense electrical storm—as if he was the storm, just barely held in check by the iron force of his will.

"I thought if I claimed to have a lover you would hate me," she said, forcing the words out, though her lips felt numb and she knew on some deep level that she could not understand, that there was no going back from this admission. This was new ground, shaky and insecure.

And still she continued on, face to face, more naked and more terrified than she could ever remember being before though she still wore her clothes.

"And I thought if you hated me," she managed to say, "You would let me go."

Something seemed to shimmer between them, bright and sharp, and he very nearly smiled. He moved closer to her, pulling a curl between his fingers and tucking it behind her ear. She was sure she saw something sad and resigned move through him before he laid a trail of soft kisses along her jaw.

He does not believe me, she thought in a dawning kind of horror, and it broke her heart.

"I never had a lover," she confessed, desperate that he hear her, that he listen, that he believe her. She was as desperate he believe this truth as she had been that he believe the lie, and even as she spoke she could not quite face the reasons she was so distraught. She only felt it, deep within, like a great abyss she had been pretending for years did not exist at all. "I made it up."

He looked up then, his eyes gleaming with a bone-deep satisfaction, bright and hard and triumphant. His mouth curved into a stark, male smile that made her shudder deep within.

"Believe me," he said, a ruthless heat in his voice, his gaze, his skin against hers, "I know."

"But…" she breathed, her voice catching in her throat, her mind a sudden tumult of 'how?' and 'when?' and 'why?' but he only laughed. It was a resoundingly wolfish sound, and she could not help the way she shuddered around him.

Then he began to move.

Later, Bethany could not pinpoint the moment she let go—the moment she stopped desperately trying to cling to the shreds of the persona she had built around Leo's absence and allowed herself instead to sink into the overwhelming, devastating reality of his presence, his body, his clever hands.

Leo made love to her with shattering intensity and ruthless, focused thoroughness. He stripped them both of all their clothes until they were naked in the sun, and then he fed her with his own fingers, olives and cheeses, salted meats and sweet grapes, and washed it down with wine and kisses.

Then he took her again, making her fall apart over and over, until she could hardly remember who she had been before that kiss of hers that had started it all again—this madness and fire, this need and heat.

When the shadows lengthened over the quiet water of the lake, Leo led her back to the castello along the same path that they had traveled that morning. Bethany felt as if years had passed since then—whole decades, perhaps, lost beneath the quiet, encompassing mastery of Leo's hands, his mouth, his hard and fascinating body.

She was not sure, she thought as he wrapped his hand around hers and tugged her with him through the vineyards, if she would recognize herself if she came face to face with the woman who had set out on this walk. She'd been so determined to play a game, so sure that game would change Leo—never dreaming how deeply it would change *her*.

But she pushed that thought away because she had no other choice. He was too demanding, too enticing, and she could not seem to stop herself from responding to his smallest caress, his barest glance. And, if she was honest, she did not want to stop herself. She did not want to stop at all.

At some point, when the enchantment of the green and gold fields had worn away and he was not there to ensnare her with his rich, dark gaze, she might have to worry about that. *But not today*, she told herself, repeating it like a litany.

When they returned to the castello, Bethany was not surprised when he was pulled aside by the usual collection of aides and servants, all of them anxious to speak to him. She climbed to her chamber and ran a hot bath in the deep tub that stood before the high windows of her expansive private bathroom.

Feeling as if she was in a dream, she pulled off the clothes he had so recently put on her, her hands trembling slightly as she remembered his method of dressing her—his mouth against the tender underside of her breasts as he smoothed her bra into place, his fingers exploring every curve, every secret, making each and every one his. She felt a deep shuddering inside of her; she could not stop herself from shivering, though she knew she was not cold.

She knew it was him: the fever of Leo Di Marco, the flush of him still heating her skin. It was the same sorcery he had always wielded over her, rendering her his slave, desperate to do or say anything that would make him touch her, take her, bring her screaming and sobbing to the completion only he could provide.

She should be horrified with herself, with what she had let happen—with what she had made happen. She knew that, could see it objectively, as if from a great distance.

She stood naked as the tub filled, and let the bath salts run through her fingers into the foamy water. She understood that she should be appalled that there was not a single square inch of her body that he had not touched, not one part of her he had not claimed beneath the canopy of the Italian sky. She raised her arms to clip her heavy curls up on the back of her head and winced slightly. She could feel him still, in the slight aches in sensitive areas that were somehow more arousing than painful; in the ecstatic, left-over shivering that she could not control or deny.

That she did not want to control. That she did not want to deny.

Whatever that made her, she did not want to know.

She had just settled into the hot, silky water, letting out a blissful sigh and tipping her head back against the high porcelain edge of the tub, when something prickled across her skin like a breeze. She opened her eyes, not at all surprised to see him in the doorway, his dark eyes shadowed.

She thought he might speak, or that she should, but neither of them moved for a long moment. She felt the steam rise around her, heating her face, making her curls tighten and bounce. But she could not look away from him.

She could not, it seemed, do anything at all but gaze at this man, helpless, as her body reacted to him in the same, predictable manner it always had. As if he had not spent the afternoon having her again and again in a variety of clever and devastating ways. Her body did not seem to care. It only wanted more.

Bethany understood something then, something that seemed to drop through her like a stone while he stood there before her.

It had always been like this—this unquenchable thirst for him, this explosive passion whenever they'd touched. She remembered that shameful night in Toronto, the night she had held up for years as the very lowest point of her life, and realized that she had needed to think of it that way. Not because they had both been so angry, but because she had needed to demonize the sexual connection between them in order to think past it, in order to figure out who she might be without it. Because when he was near her she lost the ability to think at all.

She must have known, on some level, that to demonize it the way she had was the only way she was likely to survive the loss of it, of him, for so long.

She still did not dare think of why that was. She still shied away from the simple truth that her body knew, had always known, that moved through her, illuminating her.

Not today, she thought fiercely. It would be too much, that level of self-awareness. She could not quite do it. She would not allow it.

She opened her mouth to speak, but stopped when he moved. He came to stand beside the tub, still looking down at her, that same simmering awareness lighting up his dark gaze, making his sensual mouth move into something approaching a smile.

She found she could not tear her eyes away from him. She stopped trying.

He pulled the tight black T-shirt over his

head, tossing it carelessly to the floor. Bethany let her gaze travel over his rock-hard pectoral muscles, the tantalizing indentation between them, the ridged expanse of his abdomen. She let out a small sound when he stripped off the jeans as well, kicking them out of his way so that he stood fully naked and indescribably beautiful before her.

She could only stare. He was pure, masculine perfection, lethal grace and tightly controlled strength, and she wanted to touch him and taste him all over again.

"Move over," he ordered her with a regal tilt of his jaw in a tone that expected instant compliance. That demanded it.

She knew she should object. She knew she should set her ground rules, define her boundaries. She knew she should demand her space— she knew that she should want the space from him she ought to demand. But she did not say a word. Not now, she told herself, her own private prayer. Not today.

She sat forward so he could sink down behind her in the tub that had been built for precisely this purpose. She sighed in a contentment she opted not to question when he pulled her back against the wall of his chest, settling her between his thighs, bringing his strong, hard arms around her.

The water lapped against her breasts. She could not tell which was hotter—the steaming bath or his silk-and-steel skin against hers. His hardness pressed against the small of her back, making her core throb and ache.

When she tipped her head back against his shoulder, she saw something she could not quite define flash across his face. It made something deep inside of her shift, like a tectonic plate deep beneath the ground. Grief turned to something else, something less raw, more smooth. But before she could do more than note it he fit his mouth to hers.

Soft. Sweet. The fire raged anew.

Not today, she thought. Not today.

And then she stopped thinking altogether.

CHAPTER ELEVEN

Leo could not quite put his finger on the complicated emotions that held him in such a tight grip that it bordered on the uncomfortable.

He sat in yet another tedious meeting in the suite of rooms in the castello's west wing that he used as his corporate offices when he was in Felici. He lounged behind the massive desk that his father had bought as a match for his grand ego, and knew that he looked every inch the prince, as he ought to. He had been raised to wield his own magnificence as a weapon, and he had long done so without thought. He did not want to investigate why the mantle of it seemed so ill-fitting today. As if it was no longer his second skin, indistinguishable from his own.

The meeting should not have been tedious. There had been a time when the thrill of figuring out how best to beat a rival's offer, or managing to pull together a deal in the eleventh hour, would have kept him high on adrenaline and triumph for days.

He had never involved himself in the kind of extreme adventures that attracted so many of his wealthy peers, because he could not risk himself or the Di Marco legacy. He had therefore contented himself instead with the drama of high finance—the greatest poker game in the world, with the highest stakes—and it had always worked.

Yet today, even that familiar thrill seemed to have lost its appeal. He knew that Bethany was somewhere in the castello—not in Canada, as she had been. Not across the planet. Not even so terribly angry with him any longer. She was somewhere close and, more than that, agreeable.

He knew that she was nearby, and that was what thrilled him—not these papers, these debates, these strategies that he found so unaccountably boring these days. He knew that he could walk out of this meeting, go to her and he could have her. It would be as easy as a look, a touch. As simple as their presence in the same room.

He could, as he had done yesterday, simply enter the chamber she happened to be in, tumble her to one of the soft, plush carpets and be inside of her before she had time to greet him properly. He grew hard merely thinking about it.

He scowled at the sheaf of documents in front of him, trying to make sense of the financial portfolio before him when he could hardly make sense of himself. It wasn't the sex that was affecting him this way—though he was not above feeling deeply satisfied that, even after all of the time they'd been apart, he was capable of driving Bethany absolutely wild. Driving them both wild.

It was not that at all. It was…the rest of it.

A week had passed, then several more days, and Bethany had made no move to leave; she had not so much as mentioned their divorce. She had not even asked after the court as she had when she had first arrived. Leo wanted to view that as a victory, but somehow he could not.

She shared his meals, his bed. She shared her delectable body with a delight and an enthusiasm that he found alternately humbling and exciting. She talked to him. She laughed with him. There were no tantrums, no tears, no rages, not even the barbed exchanges he had come to expect since seeing her again in Toronto.

She was, in short, everything he had always imagined she could be, as if their tumultuous eighteen months of marriage three years ago had simply been a bad dream they had woken from together.

It should have been blissful—it was blissful—yet it was not, somehow, enough.

Leo could not rid himself of the feeling of unease that never quite left him—the sense that they were living on borrowed time, that there was a clock ticking, for all that he could neither hear it nor see it. It was the far-away look in her eyes sometimes when she thought he was not watching her. It was the sadness he sometimes sensed in her, though she would always smile when he said her name and pretend she did not know what he meant when he asked what troubled her.

He knew she was holding great parts of herself in reserve, and he told himself that was why he felt this edginess, this undercurrent of disquiet. It was at odds with the deep sense of contentment he sometimes felt when she was curled around him in the night. He felt as if he could never get enough of the feel of her softness next to him, the sound of her breathing in the dark room, the scent of her lustrous curls draped across his chest.

He felt. Perhaps that was why he felt that edge inside.It was so unusual. Not new, exactly, for this was exactly why he had married her. How had he managed to forget? This had been what had happened in Hawaii, what had brought them here in the first place. He had looked at her, touched her and it was as if he'd been reborn. Made new.

With Bethany, he was aware of himself as a man in a way he was with no one else. He was not the *Principe di Felici*. He was not the heir to the Di Marco fortune and executor of its storied legacy. He was simply a man. A man who wanted her, who she wanted in return, as if nothing else mattered. As if only that mattered.

He had hated that he'd felt this way. He could remember it all now with a clarity that had somehow deserted him during the years she had been gone. He remembered how bizarre he had found his own feelings when he'd returned to Italy, having acted out of character for the first time in his life.

He had felt as if he had dishonored himself. He had not known how to act like the man who had fallen so in love with her, so in love that he'd forgotten the history that had made him who he was until he was immersed once again in the seat of that history. He had instead tried to pretend that the man who had been so alive, so accessible, so vulnerable in the soft Hawaiian night had never existed.

Worse, he had tried to make her into the woman he had been meant to marry, the stiff and formal automaton that she had never been and could never be. He had tried to make the two of them into the image of the marriages he'd witnessed his whole life—fake and bloodless society arrangements, all manners and materialism, convenience and practicality. Why had he been surprised when she could not handle it? What had he expected?

The outer door to his office swung open then and Leo glanced up as one of his fleet of secretaries walked in. He could see out into the antechamber, and felt that spike of desire pound through him when he saw that Bethany was standing there, smiling at one of the attorneys who had left earlier to take a telephone call. He snuck a look at his watch and saw that it was nearing noon, when he had planned to meet her for lunch.

She looked fresh and pretty, her curls spilling toward her shoulders from a high ponytail, the dark gloss of her hair seeming to shine against the pale peach cashmere of the turtleneck sweater she wore. Her dark brown trousers clung to her curves, and made him think of more private venues for their meal than the excursion they'd planned into the village.

But when she turned toward his door her

gaze met his for a split second across the ante-chamber and the spacious inner-office before the same secretary walked out and closed the door behind her.

The split second had been enough. Leo felt the force of her gaze as if it still seared into him through the heavy wooden door. Tortured. Bitter. Despairing.

Furious.

And he knew then exactly what he had feared, exactly what he had felt floating around them, undermining all the seeming perfection of their reunion: this moment.

This was what he'd been attempting to avoid all along.

Because he knew what the damned lawyer must have told her. He knew exactly what could put that horrible look on the face that had been soft and shining when he'd left her this morning.

He had taken his biggest gamble yet, he realized, and if that expression was anything to go by Leo Di Marco had finally lost. He had lost and this loss, he realized with a sudden flare of deep certainty, he could not tolerate.

He could not. He would not.

"Excuse me, gentlemen," he said, cutting off the consultant who was still speaking. He rose to his feet. Because he was the prince, no one argued—no one even commented. They merely stood respectfully. "Something has come up."

Then, with a growing sense of something he refused to call panic, but which shot through him too fast and too slick, he went after her.

He was a liar.

He was still no more than a liar.

Bethany could not breathe. She could not breathe, and she could not seem to stop making that choking sound in the back of her throat as she hurtled herself down the long, history-laden hallway that seemed to shrink around her as she moved. Oppressive, not beautiful. Dark, not graceful. A prison, not a castle—all over again.

How could she have forgotten how ruthless he was? How could she have done the one thing she had known better than to do and fallen right back into his arms, his bed? It was as if he touched her and she immediately contracted some kind of amnesia. What had she been thinking? Had she been thinking?

All the while, he had lied to her.

She reached her chamber and threw open the door, her breath coming in shallow, desperate pants. She was a fool, such a naïve little fool, even now. It was not her youth or her inexperience this time. It was him.

It was Leo, who had never intended to let her go. Who had talked her into coming to Italy simply because he'd grown tired of waiting for her to return of her own volition, because he wanted her here for whatever complicated reason of his own. And he was the prince—he did as he pleased. His wish was her command. Her stomach heaved.

But what other explanation could there be? The lawyer had told her the sickening truth about Italian divorces outside Leo's office: both spouses had to appear in court and declare they wished to separate. And only after three years of legal separation had passed could divorce be considered, much less granted.

"But I explained all of this to the prince…" the man had stammered apologetically. "Weeks ago."

She had no doubt at all that he had done precisely that.

Which could only mean one thing, she thought as she staggered into her bedchamber and then stood there, her head spinning around and around: Leo had brought her here under false pretenses. He had known the laws of his own country; of this, Bethany had no doubt. He had always intended to use her body against her, to lull her into a false sense of security.

She heard herself let out a low sound, a kind

of sob, and then she bit it back, the pain too great, the anger leaving her as suddenly as it had crashed into her.

She was not his puppet. She was not some kind of marionette that he directed at his whim. She had chosen to kiss him at the lakeside. She had done this to herself, in full possession of her faculties, for all the good they had done her. She had abandoned herself as totally as she had years ago—as completely as everyone else had abandoned her over the years.

Her mother, who had died when she was so young, who she had never known. Her father, who had been wracked with grief, then so weak, then so ill, before he died. Leo, who had left her so alone when she had not known herself at all, much less him. But, above all, she had abandoned herself. She had lost herself again and again, and it was this that she thought she might never forgive. Leo was merely the catalyst.

This was no more than her latest great betrayal—the latest heartbreak she had perpetrated on herself with her own shocking inability to keep herself safe as she should, as any adult would. Leo's manipulations were almost beside the point. This was, after all, who he was, and she'd known it full well. She'd had no illusions at all about what sort of man he was, had she?

So why was she so astonished? Why did it hurt so much that she could not manage to breathe as she should? Why did she feel so…bruised?

It didn't matter who was to blame, she told herself, pushing past the anguish. It only underscored what she had always known: she could not stay here. She should never have come here. She had known better, and yet she had done it anyway.

And she even knew why.

It was like a sickness, she thought, a great wave of despair crashing over her, so hard it nearly took her to her knees. She moved over to the great four-poster bed and leaned against it, her hands loath to touch the linens where she had lain with him, over him, where he had brought her to such great heights with his hands, his mouth, that all-seeing gaze and boundless need.

And all of it part of this lie, she thought, miserable. The lie she should have known he would tell, because this was who he was. Why did it hurt so much to have her worst suspicions confirmed?

But she knew. She loved him. Despite everything, she was in love with him.

She rubbed her hands over her face, but the uncomfortable and ugly truth did not dissipate. The love, fierce and tough and uncompromising, remained. It was why she had stayed in that house in Toronto, rattling around like a wraith. It was why she had let him talk her into coming here. It was why. It was that silken, unbreakable thread of hope that could not let him go. She did not want to love him, but she did. She still did. She always had.

She had loved him since she'd first laid eyes on him, wet and glistening in the Hawaiian sun, and nothing had ever altered that love. Nothing had changed it or diminished it. She had adored him, hated him, feared him, blamed him—and still she loved him.

These past days had been a fantasy of all they could have been; he had been, at last, the man she remembered from Hawaii so long ago. The man she had thrown away all she'd known to follow heedlessly across the globe. But even knowing now what she had not wanted to suspect—even now, she loved him.

There was no one else for her. She faced the truth of that, and managed not to flinch. There would be no 'moving on', no 'getting over it.' There was only Leo. He had broken her heart so many times she had stopped expecting anything else. Yet still she could feel the way she loved him swell in her, dance through her veins and slide deep into her bones. Even now, when she wondered how she would ever survive this moment. Even now, when she was not even sure she wanted to survive it.

She loved him, but he was still playing his games. He was still playing lord of the manor, the presumptuous prince. He was still manipulative and deceiving, patronizing and cruel. She had stopped questioning why she should love a man like that, who seemed sometimes to be so different, so good, so noble.

But there was no use in questioning it. She loved him, but that did not mean she had to live with him and let him move her around like one more pawn on his chess board. She knew she could bear almost anything, but not that.

Something rolled through her then, something hot and arid—her love, her history and her heart so broken it could never be repaired. She straightened from the bed and marched over to the dressing room door. Wrenching it open, she stalked inside, yanked her roller-bag out and tossed it on the bench that ran along the wall. It would not take long to pack—after all, she had come with so little and she would leave as she'd always sworn she would: with nothing he had given her. With only what was hers.

You will be perfectly fine, she told herself, repeating the phrase again and again, though she knew better than to believe it. But she would survive. The worst had already happened three years ago—she had already lived without him, had already had to accept that he did not and could not love her in the way she loved him.

She could do it again. She would do it again. And, if it hurt her worse this time somehow—because she had expected she would keep herself safe and armed with all she knew—well, she had years and years ahead of her to explore that particular shame.

"What the hell are you doing?"

His voice came from the door, low and fierce. She did not look up. She did not trust either one of them.

"I think you know," she said in a quiet, controlled voice that cost her bits of her soul.

She tossed her jeans into the bag and then zipped it shut. Who cared what she left behind? She wanted to leave. She needed to leave, immediately. Before he could tell her more lies she would want so desperately to believe. Before she could betray herself further.

"You are leaving," he said, as if he could not believe it, as if his eyes must be deceiving him. As if—as usual—she was the villain in this piece. "You are packing up and running off again?"

She turned on him then and was slightly

taken back when she saw an unexpected wildness in his dark eyes, a kind of raw fury she had never seen before. She had no idea what it meant, and so plunged ahead.

"Did you know?" she asked, her voice clipped. She glared at him, forcing herself to be fierce, refusing to show him the agony inside, much less that terrible, doomed love for him that made her act like such a colossal fool. "Did you know that we would have to register our separation and then wait three years? And did you convince me to come here anyway, knowing that I thought we could divorce immediately? Did you manipulate me in that way, Leo?"

His lips pressed together into a hard line. His eyes burned but he did not speak. One moment passed. Then another.

Bethany did not realize how much she had hoped he would have an explanation until he failed to offer one. She let out the breath she had not been aware she was holding.

"Well," she said unevenly, and it cost her not to show how deeply his silence hurt her. "There we are."

"Did I drag you here against your will, Bethany?" he asked fiercely, his features harsh with something like pain. "Did I kidnap you like the savage you love to tell yourself I am? Did I lay a single finger upon you before you asked me to do so?"

"No, of course not," she said bitterly, the pain of all their years so heavy on her heart, that she thought her knees might give way. Part of her wanted to collapse beneath it, to be done with it finally. To be at some kind of peace. But she could not allow that, and she knew it. She felt her lips twist into something rueful. "You are a saint."

"You are my wife," he said.

"What does that mean?" she asked, hearing her own voice shake but not knowing what she could do to stop it. "You still do not have the right to treat me this way—like an asset you must manage, a pawn you must maneuver around according to your own Byzantine rules! I am a person, Leo. I have feelings. And I am tired of you treading them into dust beneath your feet!"

"You have feelings?" he demanded in a kind of furious amazement. "You dare to stand there, one foot out of the door, your suitcase packed, and talk to me of your feelings?"

"I do not want a lake from you some day once I finally *do my duty*," she threw at him, barely able to see him through the sheen of tears she desperately wanted not to shed, to keep hidden. But then they were streaming down her cheeks, and she could see the look on his face—as if she'd hit him with something much too hard in his gut—yet she could not seem to stop. "I do not want your parents' marriage. I won't do it, Leo. You cannot make me do it!"

"I love you!" he bellowed. She did not know what was more astonishing—the words themselves or the tone in which they were delivered.

Leo—shouting? Leo—with that color splashed across his high cheekbones and eyes too wild to be his? Love? He had not mentioned love since those heady early days so lost to them now.... She could not take it in. She could not absorb it, make sense of it.

Though that traitorous part of her, that silver thread, pulled taut. Hoped.

"I love you," he said again more quietly, but somehow it had all the same kick and power of the louder version. It seemed to rip into her, ricocheting inside of her like a bullet and doing as much damage.

He stepped further into the room. She could see that he was not the man she knew—not the perfectly groomed, perfectly pressed prince. The man in front of her looked slightly out of breath, and ever so slightly disheveled—as if he'd run after her, which was impossible. As if he had not stopped to smooth his clothes back into line, which was unlikely.

As if he was finally telling the truth, a small voice whispered, and her heart began to kick painfully against her ribs.

"You…" She could not repeat what he'd said. It hurt too much. It made her yearn for things he had proven, time and again, he could not give. She shook her head. "If you loved me, you would not spend so much time trying to manipulate me. Surely you must know that?"

"Let me tell you what I know about love," he said, his voice ragged, not his at all. It seemed to strike her directly in the heart, paralyzing her. "Nothing," he snapped. "Not one damn thing, Bethany. No one was at all concerned with teaching me about something I was never expected to experience."

She wanted to go to him, to hold him, to mourn with him for the things that had been done to him, but she could not. She ached for him, for both of them, but she could not move. Neither toward him, nor away.

"Your parents treated you abominably," she said in a low voice. "But that does not give you the right to do these things to me. You cannot truly believe that it is okay. You cannot. If you thought you were in the right, you would not have hidden it from me."

"It never crossed my mind to do anything but my duty," he continued in that same rough, almost angry tone. "And then there you were. You were nothing like the woman I was expected to choose. You were too warm, too alive, and you expected the same from me. You saw me as a man. Just a man. And I loved you when I had never known I could love at all."

"And look what we have done with it," she said, her voice so rough she hardly recognized it. She used her fists to dash the tears away from her eyes and could not even hate herself for showing that weakness. "Look what we've become."

"Bethany," he said, his voice harsh; she could see to her amazement that he was pleading. This man, who only issued orders. This man, who did not know how to bend at all.

But she had already bent too much. She had bent and twisted and tied herself into knots, and she trusted neither one of them anymore. How could she? He had lied to her and, worse, she had lied to herself. She could not handle herself around this man. She never could. How many times must she prove this same failing to herself, in ever more catastrophic ways?

Three years ago she had dissolved into incoherent rages and tantrums, trying desperately to reach him. This time, she had simply dissolved into him as if she had no other existence of her own, as if her return to this place completely deleted all that had gone before.

She loved him, but he was no good for her, and she was never going to become the person whom he should have married. Hadn't they learned all of this long ago? Why were they still here, still fighting, over the same futile ground?

"I do not want a lake," she said again, not sure why she could not let go of it.

She imagined the pretty stretch of grass where she'd found herself so enchanted that she'd lost her head and surrendered herself to him once more. It was the bait, perhaps, to the pretty little trap this life could be, but she did not have to accept that particular cage.

Who would she be if she stayed here? Leo's mother, whose name was never mentioned as if she had never existed outside of her prescribed roles? A woman who had merited a show of respect in the form of that lake, but no true respect at all? And no love.

Certainly no love. The woman's only son spoke of it as if it was an alien notion, profoundly foreign to him. How could she live with that?

"I am not willing to relive your parents' marriage," she told him then, aware that he was watching her with that terrible look on his beautiful face, as if she was killing him. As if she was doing it with her own hands. It made her ache, but she could not let herself stop. "I'm not willing to simply accept unhappiness."

"Why are you so certain that we will be unhappy?" he demanded, his voice still so raw. "Have you been unhappy since you came here?"

"It's like that lake…" she began.

"I will dredge it and pave it over with concrete, if that will make you happy," he gritted out, temper crackling in his voice. "If that will keep you from mentioning it again—as if I built it myself!"

"It doesn't matter how happy we are, or think we are, because there is always something rotten underneath," she managed to say. "There is always another game, another lie. We cannot do this. It has been five excruciating years and we have proven repeatedly that we cannot do it, Leo. We simply cannot."

It was as if the pain was another entity, a vast sea, an agony both acute and dull ringing in her ears and cramping her belly. It seemed to fill the room, shining from Leo's drawn, ragged features and the very salt in the tears that she could not seem to stop, the tears that slipped down her cheeks unheeded.

"Then what do you want?" he asked starkly.

Bethany did not mistake the question for another shot in their long battle. It was a deeply serious question. He looked at her as if he could see into her, as if he knew the things she still kept hidden. As if he wanted to see everything.

She thought for a brief moment that she could do it—that she could say she loved him too and let that sit there between them. That she could let herself be that vulnerable, that honest, that open. That she could risk it—risk everything.

But all those empty years... All the times she had said she loved him and he had merely smiled and then used her desperation to make her do his bidding. All the nights she had tossed and turned, alone and ravaged with this terrible grief, tortured by the love she would have cut out of her own flesh if she'd been able to.

How could she trust this man with her heart when she could not trust herself with it? How could she possibly admit to that much vulnerability when she was already so shaky?

Nothing good can come of this, she told herself bleakly, staring at him, her tears making his dark coffee eyes seem to shimmer and glow. Nothing ever has.

"Tell me what you want," he said gruffly, as if it hurt him too. "Tell me and it is yours."

She wanted so many things. She always had. But she was too beaten, too bruised by all of their epic and painful failures. She had given up too much and she was so afraid that she had no more left to give. She could not do it anymore. In that moment she wanted some semblance of peace more than she wanted anything else— even him.

"I want a divorce," she whispered, and saw his eyes go cold, his mouth tauten, his face pale.

But it was better to break what was left of her heart right now than to hand it to him and watch him smash it into dust again and again until nothing was left, not even that thread of hope that had kept her going all these long years.

She told herself it had to be.

CHAPTER TWELVE

LEO found himself standing in her bedchamber,
the ancient room seeming to whirl around him.
His heart was too loud in his ears and his chest,
and he could not seem to force a full breath.

He could not believe the finality he had heard
in Bethany's voice, had seen stamped on her
face. He could not believe that after all of this—
all they had been through, all they clearly still
felt for each other—she still wanted to divorce
him. He could not accept that she wanted to
leave him. Everything in him rebelled at the
thought!

He had told her he loved her, and it had not
moved her at all, when the same words had
once transported her entirely—made her smile
and laugh and shine from within. He did not
know where to put that sad reality, how to keep
it from tearing at him.

If you loved me, you would not spend so
much time trying to manipulate me, she had

said. Her words still echoed in his head, sounding like an uncomfortable truth. *Look what we've become.*

He felt his hands clench into fists at his sides.

She did not want a lake, and he did not want to be a man like his father who would build such a monument to something he had never felt. He did not want her trapped and miserable, unhappy and dutiful. He did not want this woman who had wrecked him and exalted him, sometimes with the same small smile, to end up like his own mother. He did not want her to transform herself into the kind of woman he'd been supposed to marry. He did not want any part of the life he'd been lucky to be banished from as a small boy. Was that what he wanted for his own children?

He knew he did not.

And he also knew, though he wished he did not, that it was his pride that wanted to force her to stay, his pride that wanted to keep her no matter what it was she said she wanted. He might not believe that she was as finished with him as she claimed to be, but it was only his pride that would force her to confront that, wasn't it?

He had lived his life in service of his pride for far too long, he thought then. Because once he set it aside, all he could see was the expression on Bethany's pretty face, pale and streaked with tears. Did he love her so little that he could keep her here, his prisoner, when she wanted to leave? Did he want her close to him more than he wanted her happy?

He detested himself for how long it took to answer that question, for how agonizing it was to come to the only possible conclusion.

That was the kind of man he was, he thought bitterly. The kind of man she accused him of being. That was exactly who he was to her, and had always been: autocratic, conniving, manipulative. Just as she'd thrown at him, time and again—but he had excused it all away because he had told himself it was all about duty and obligation, when, in truth, he had simply wanted her.

Here. Now. For ever.

He had seen her and he had never looked at another woman again. He had never wanted anyone else. Only Bethany. He simply wanted her with him in whatever way he could have her, because without her he feared he would disappear forever beneath the crushing weight of his own vast history, his family's legacy.

He let out a breath and let it roll through him, the truth he had fought so hard, so long, to suppress, even from himself.

She was the only one who had ever seen him

simply as a man. But she could not be happy if she was with him. This was finally clear to him. It was killing her—and he could not stand by and let something hurt her so badly, even if what was hurting her was him.

He had to let her go. He did not know how he would do it when every single instinct he possessed screamed that he must prevent this very thing at all costs—he only knew he had no other choice.

Bethany did not realize that she had sunk to the floor until she looked up to see Leo standing before her, a strange and unreadable expression on his face. She stared at him, aware then that she was on her knees. She had no idea how that had happened. She had told him she wanted a divorce, he had walked away from her and it had been over.

She had known, with some kind of primitive instinct that seemed to emanate from deep inside of her, that they had finally snapped that thread of hope. It was finally broken. They had finally ended this thing between them, whatever it was, and she was free. Free to go, free to live—free.

And it felt like dying.

"Did you fall?" he asked in a voice that sounded far away, as if it was a stranger's.

Or perhaps she had become the stranger, having cut the thread that tied them together. Perhaps that tiny little shred of hope had been the only thing that had bound them, after all. She tried to wet her lips, to speak, but nothing came out.

"Are you unwell?" he asked, his elegant brow furrowing as he moved closer. She had to blink to bring him into focus, and that was when she realized that tears still coursed down her cheeks unchecked.

"I want to walk out of here," she managed to say in a whisper that seemed to tear at her throat. She felt the hot sting of her tears, the clog of emotion in her chest, the threat of deep sobs from low in her abdomen. "I want to be free...of all of this."

A stark emptiness washed across his face, hurting her as surely as if he'd struck her, even when she would have thought that she could not hurt any further—that it was not physically possible.

"I told you that I love you and I mean it, Bethany," he said in a low, quiet, awful voice, his powerful hands in fists at his sides, his dark eyes bleak. "And I will love you enough to let you go, if I must."

His mouth flattened into that grim line. He looked...defeated, this strong, unbreakable man. It made Bethany feel like shattered glass, all jagged shards and fine dust scattered across the floor. It made her want to rewind, erase, do whatever it took to make him Leo again.

"If that is what you want," he said.

It rang in the air like a vow, and she believed him. He would let her go. He would do it. Only moments ago, she had known that was precisely what she wanted. She had been deeply hurt, but sure. Certain. Leo was finally acquiescing, and this time she knew that he was not playing one of his games. They had moved far past that.

This time, he meant it. Which meant that all she had to do was stand and walk out of this place, head high, heart battered, perhaps, but free—just as she'd wanted to be for so long.

All she needed to do was rise, climb to her feet and start for the door. Start the rest of her life as she'd believed she wanted to do for so long.

Stand up! she ordered herself, desperate.

But she could not seem to do it.

"I do not know how to let you go," he said, his voice darker than she had ever heard it, laced with all the pain and sorrow she knew was inside of her, spilling out of her. "But I will do it, Bethany. I promise you."

It seemed to reverberate deep in her heart. It made her feel weighted to the floor, heavy like a stone, when she kept telling herself she should feel lighter, should fly, should cast aside the shackles she had always believed he'd placed on her and make for the sun.

Was this how it ended for them? Was this how it felt?

But her legs refused to work. Her hands were clasped together before her as if she were praying, and she could not force herself to wrench her gaze away from his. She was not sure she was even breathing. Time seemed to stand still, fold in on itself, and all she knew was that sorrow in her heart and the way it reflected back at her from his bittersweet gaze.

She had cut that last silver line of hope, of the dream of him, and without it, she knew suddenly, with a deep certainty that seemed to echo inside of her and grow louder with every passing second, she was as unknowable to herself as he was without the great long parade of his history.

He was her history. He had made her as surely as she had made herself; they were entwined and entangled, and she did not know how to exist without it. Without him. She could as soon exist without air.

Thinking that, she released the breath she had been holding and inhaled deeply, as if for the first time.

"I cannot seem to leave you," she whispered then, something like grief washing through her as if it was overflowing from within, as if it was a poison, as if it had to get out. "I have been trying to do it for years, and this time even my legs have given out on me."

"I will carry you wherever you want to go, if you wish it," he said gruffly, and she could see that he meant it, this difficult man, however little he wished her to leave.

He would do it because he was honorable, for all she had longed to believe otherwise. He was not his father. He was not a monster. He was, perhaps, as conflicted and confused as she had always been.

Then she could not hold any of it at bay any longer—the sweltering heat and storm of all that sorrow, all that pain, all their years and wars and battles and passions—and she bent over with the force of it, sobbing it out into the plush carpet beneath her.

"Come now," he murmured, coming closer.

But still she wept, as if she would never stop, as if she was only beginning, as if she could make sense of the past five years through the salt of her tears.

"Bethany," he said softly as his arms went around her and lifted her. "Please."

But she sobbed against the wide wall of his

chest, his scent and heat enveloping her like an embrace, warming her, caressing her, keeping her safe while the storm raged on.

"Come, luce mio; do not cry like this," he murmured close to her ear, pressing a kiss against the flushed skin of her cheek, soothing her the only way he could. "I beg you."

But she could not seem to stop. Not when he lapsed into crooning, comforting Italian. Not when he carried her to the window seat in the bedchamber and settled her on his lap, holding her close and murmuring into her ear. She cried and cried, and she could not make herself stop it any more than she had been able to make herself stand up and walk out the door.

Instead, she simply let him hold her.

"This is my fault," he said when she had been quiet against him, in his arms, for a time. Bethany tilted her head back and searched his face. He held her close to his chest, but for once she did not worry that this made her appear the child. She felt…comforted by the steady beat of his heart. By his warmth. By his muscled strength surrounding her.

"If there is fault," she said, her voice raspy in the aftermath of the storm that had shaken her, her eyes feeling swollen and bruised. "Then there is enough to go around."

"I am the perfect prince," he said, his tone heavily sardonic, and for once she knew he aimed it at himself. "I have spent my life practicing, so one should hope I've succeeded at it after all these years." His eyes blazed at her, alight with a kind of determination she had never seen before. "But I am not much of a man."

"I love you," she said unevenly.

The fear was gone, wept away. She was washed clean. Only the truth remained, shining hot and bright inside her like a beacon. Like something profoundly, life-alteringly simple. She loved him. What else mattered?

She sat forward, turning so she could face him on the window seat. "That does not mean it is not complicated. That it is not painful. But I have always loved you."

"I know," he said, a ghost of his arrogant smile curving his sensual lips, though his eyes blazed and his face filled with an emotion that made her stomach clench. "But I did not think that mattered to you any longer."

"Of course it matters to me!" she whispered. He reached over and traced her mouth with one long, tapered finger, elegant as the rest of him. He smoothed his fingertip along the bow of her upper lip, the curve of her lower lip, and Bethany shivered slightly as that same familiar fire scorched her from within, as it always did. Always. Leo smiled slightly and drew his hand away.

Bethany stared at him for a long moment, as if she could see the answer to all of their problems tattooed across his beautiful, regal, beloved face. She was not sure what she felt, or how. All she knew was that once again she could not take the final step that would separate her from him. She could not do it. And every second that she did not leave, that she let him hold her, that she breathed in and felt him do the same beside her, that resilient little thread of hope stretched out between them. And grew thicker. Tougher. It would be that much harder to break the next time.

Maybe, a little voice whispered inside her heart, it is not supposed to break at all.

She had wanted him to be all things to her, when he had wanted the chance to be no more than a man. She had wanted him to keep her safe, but there was nothing safe about loving like this—so deep and so hard that it had altered her completely, changed her, made her into someone she had not recognized for years. She had feared it for so long, fought it, fought him, desperate to keep herself from disappearing in him. Because that was what she'd always been so scared would happen if she succumbed to the power of her feelings. He was so much bigger than life, so much more than she had ever dared dream... Of course she had thought he would consume her whole.

But what if that was not what happened at all?

Today she had seen Leo as she never had before. Perhaps he had always been this way and she had been too overawed by him to note it, but today she realized that she had the power to hurt him as much as he had hurt her. It did not make her happy or proud of herself. But, as she sat and looked at him, she felt that shifting once again, as if they sat on a fault line and the earth was readjusting itself beneath them. If he did not hold all the power, then that meant she could only disappear if she chose to let that happen. If she did it herself, to herself. But... what if she did not?

What then?

She was not a puppet, she thought, the words feeling almost nonsensical, impossible, in her own head even as they resounded like truth in her gut. But a partner. His partner.

The idea of it all but took her breath away.

"If you are leaving me," he said, his voice low and rough, his gaze intent on hers as if he was inside of her already, as if he could read her as easily as he read her body, as if he knew what she was thinking, "then you must do it soon, Bethany. I am only a man, and not a particularly decent one, I do not think. I fear my good intentions are few and far between where you are concerned."

She felt the tug in her heart, the silver string wrapping around her again and again, tying her securely to him as it always had. She understood, in a way she never had before, that she could choose.

Every moment of the day, every moment with this man, she could choose: hope or fear. One would help her fly and one would shut her down. She had spent three years in fear, all alone in that house in Toronto. She had spent all the scared and lonely nights she needed to spend. Did she really want to spend the rest of her life that way, loving this man and keeping herself apart from him because it scared her too much to be with him?

What kind of life was that?

She sat up straighter and could not look at him. She lifted up the hands that she'd kept clenched into fists while the sobs had wracked her body and she'd cried out all the years of sorrow.

"But what if I choose to stay?" she asked, her voice the barest whisper, though she saw each word hit him like an electrical bolt. His dark eyes blazed with a fierce hope she recognized. She felt it hitch in her own chest.

And then, slowly, she opened up her hands until he could see her palms and what lay in each of them—what she had scrabbled to find in the pocket of the purse where she'd secreted them. What she had held on to even as she fell to her knees.

In one palm lay a simple platinum band. In the other, an exquisite sapphire ring.

"I was given to understand you got rid of them," Leo said with an echo of his usual arch amusement, but he picked up the rings, holding them in his much bigger hands as if he was seeing them for the first time. As if he had not selected them himself from the Cartier boutique in Waikiki. As if he had not slid them onto her trembling fingers while she'd cried tears of joy through a smile so wide it had made her jaw ache.

"I refused to wear them," Bethany admitted, looking at him and pushing through the cloud of fear—because what was a little more vulnerability at this point? What was left to protect, if she lost him and herself? "But I could not be without them."

It was one more truth she had ignored. One more clue. One more part of a deep, abiding and painful love she had given up on, called hopeless, but had never quite managed to let go.

His eyes met hers then and Bethany felt exactly the same way she'd felt when they'd married on that private beach in Hawaii years ago. Holy. Sacred.

Right—despite everything.

They had stripped everything away, and here they still were. She could choose to fear, or she could choose to hope. She could choose—and the truth was that her heart had chosen long ago.

It had never wavered, even when she had—especially then.

"Allow me," Leo said.

Then, just as he had so long ago, he put the rings back where they belonged. One by one, he gently slid them onto Bethany's left hand. When they were secured, he laced his fingers tight to hers and drew her hand to his mouth.

"Do we start again?" he asked, his brown eyes calm and clear but so alive. So filled with hope, with a love she thought she just might dare to believe. To return. Bethany felt his gaze move through her, down to her toes.

Such a simple question, for such a complicated endeavor. But what else could they do? They could not seem to live apart. They could not seem to leave. Perhaps it was time to see what they could build together.

"We cannot seem to end," she said, but her heart felt full, and the threads that tied her to him felt intricately knotted, tangled and tight. At last, she admitted to herself that she wanted it that way. That on some level she always had.

"Then we might as well begin," he said huskily. A new promise. "Again and again."

"Until we get it right," Bethany vowed, her voice soft and sure.

He leaned closer and pressed his mouth to hers, making it right. Lighting the great fire that had always burned within them.

Sealing the promises they'd made so long ago. Sealing their fate.

Setting them both free.

* * * * *